Praise for

Her Beauty
BURNS

"*Her Beauty Burns* by author Jenn Sadai is the second installment of her *Survivor Series*, an almost memoir-styled cautionary tale about relationships, self esteem, and domestic violence. *Her Beauty Burns* is inspiring, at times gut-wrenching, and even suspenseful. A true page-turner. My favorite yet from author Jenn Sadai.

I think there is a very important lesson tucked away in this story, and that lesson is to not necessarily give everyone the benefit of the doubt. We owe it to our own hearts, not to others, and sometimes our hearts are wrong. When friends and family tell you they are concerned, listen to them. They aren't thinking with their 'hearts,' they're thinking with their brains. I think this is so important and sometimes we are blinded because of love. What a painful, heartbreaking lesson for Katelyn, the protagonist, to learn.

Another lesson I learned from this story is how toxic people seek out people like Katelyn, who are emotionally damaged or have problems with self-esteem. Katelyn didn't pick a bad guy, and she doesn't go for the 'wrong ones.' Instead he found her. Katelyn's story is inspiring, and I feel it can help young women who are dealing with similar circumstances, perhaps before it's too late. A must read."

— APRIL L. WOOD,
Author of the *Season of the Witch Series*

Her Beauty
BURNS

Jenn Sadai

Jan-Carol
Publishing, Inc
"every story needs a book"

Cathy,
Burn
Bright
Always
Jenn Sadai

Her Beauty Burns
Jenn Sadai

Published February 2019
Little Creek Books
Imprint of Jan-Carol Publishing, Inc

ISBN: 978-1-945619-92-2
Library of Congress Control Number: 2019933582

You may contact the publisher:
Jan-Carol Publishing, Inc
PO Box 701
Johnson City, TN 37605
publisher@jancarolpublishing.com
jancarolpublishing.com

This book is dedicated to every woman
who has ever lost herself in the pursuit of love.

Letter to the Reader

Love is a powerful drug. It's easy to get swept up in a steamy romance. Burning passion can be so consuming that it blinds us to the warning signs. We don't notice there's smoke until our souls are already on fire.

Her Beauty Burns is the second book in my *Survivor Series* and delves into the emotional manipulation and warning signs of abuse. Katelyn, who was briefly introduced in *Her Own Hero*, tells the story of how her fierce confidence went up in smoke at the hands of a master manipulator.

I set several heavy goals for this story. I want it to remind women to trust their instincts, to stay true to the relationships that matter, and to know their worth is not dependent on their appearance. Most importantly, I want the reader to know that no matter how badly things go wrong in life, you can always make it right again.

Spread love always,

Jenn Sadai

Acknowledgments

My super support group grows with every book and I could never possibly name everyone who has helped me succeed. Sincere love and appreciation to Jeff Boakes, Rob Sadai, Christine Boakes, Liz Cormier, Jeremy Boakes, Shawna Boakes, Rahel Levesque, Kim Harrison, Deb Birchard, Bill Birchard, Sarah Pinsonneault, Kim Chapieski, Louise Smith, Natalie Hartleib, Jamie Lees, Melissa McCormick, and Sheryl Davies. I'm always grateful for the stunning cover design and layout by my forever friend Kim Harrison and the team at Jan-Carol Publishing, Inc.

The Pretty One

For as long as I could remember, I was always referred to as "the pretty one." My older sister Amy was the scholar who impressed teachers and brought home the stellar report cards that my parents gushed over. My younger sister Tina is known as the boy my dad never had, and she's constantly praised for her phenomenal athletic abilities.

I was simply the pretty one.

My sisters are most definitely attractive girls, and I'm not completely devoid of my sisters' skill sets. I did fairly well in school. Well, at least I was a conscientious student, up until I met the man who would eventually set my world on fire. I wasn't first in my class like Amy, but I usually ranked between second and fourth, especially in art, gym, and social sciences. I was also a track star, striving to earn a scholarship in cross country. I had the best time record at my school, and I was third in the province.

Despite my well-rounded capabilities, I only really received compliments on my appearance. People would comment on how nice I looked almost instantly; most never discovered that there's more to me than meets the eye.

Being evaluated solely on my physical shell never bothered me before the fire. I used to soak in the attention I received when I walked in a room. I would purposely move extra slow and fling my long, dark hair dramatically from my shoulders, just so that more people would notice me. I shrugged off the stream of flattery like it didn't matter, but if I'm completely honest with myself, I relished being admired for how I looked.

I was told that my face belonged on a magazine cover and I was gifted a life that most other teenage girls envied. I hung out with the popular crowd, was invited to every party, and had quite a few guys ask me out before I was even old enough to date. The constant flattery made me significantly more confident than most young teenage girls.

Now I miss my fierce confidence a whole lot more than I miss my perfect skin.

Well...maybe not quite as much as I miss having two normal-sized ears. I haven't felt confident enough to wear my hair in a ponytail or tuck it behind my ears since the fire. The melted, disfigured nub jutting out only an inch from the right side of my head still bothers me. I often wonder if having only one ear would be better than the mini-mess of flesh hiding behind my thick hair. I'm trying not to be so vain, but it's a hard habit to break.

The attention my more noticeable scars attracted was a new experience for me. I made it through the socially awkward phases of my youth unscathed. I never had a blemish to stress over or gained any substantial weight like the majority of my friends. I was blessed with physical beauty, and unlike most girls, I knew how attractive I was before I entered the judgmental war zone of high school.

My self-esteem didn't start to shrink until I was almost finished with high school. It wasn't due to any drastic change in my appearance or social status—although those changes obviously followed. Like most young women, I surrendered my self-worth to a boy, and watched silently as he shredded it into tiny pieces in the blink of an eye.

I wasn't allowed to go on an actual date until I turned sixteen. My parents would let me hang out with boys I liked, but only in group settings. There were only a couple boys I was really interested in. For the greater part of high school, there were considerably more guys vying for my attention that I couldn't be bothered to acknowledge.

Back then, there was only one guy who crossed my mind quite frequently: Ethan Tucker. He was blatantly flirtatious, genuinely charming, and universally irresistible. That's probably why he practiced his persuasive superpowers on almost every girl in school, never committing for very long to anything or anyone. I appreciated a challenge, and felt like I was enough of a catch to grab his full attention.

Ethan had dark blonde hair with long bangs that swept gently across his forehead. His pale blue eyes and fair skin were a stark contrast to his rugged dark brown Hollister bomber, faded black jeans, and worn-out Nikes. He looked innocent enough to pass for the boy next door in front of parents and teachers, while still maintaining his bad boy status with his classmates.

He knew the effect he had on the girls in my school. Ethan walked the halls liked he owned them, which was one of the reasons he stood out from the rest of the awkward wobblers. Very few boys—and even fewer girls—carried themselves with noticeable confidence. Ethan and I were the exceptions.

Surprisingly, Ethan Tucker wasn't one of the guys seeking my affection at the time. It had been months since he'd tried to sweet-talk me into some alone time. Since then, he acted more like I was invisible, and would enthusiastically chat up other girls at school right in front of me. I assumed he was trying to make me jealous, or possibly that my prior rejections had convinced him that I was out of his league, so he'd stopped trying. That's why I thought it was necessary for me to make the first move.

Our school had an after-hours dance coming up, and I planned on boldly asking him to dance with me. I assumed he'd respect a girl who had the confidence to offer the initial invitation. It would be the first time I'd pursued a guy in the hopes of him becoming my boyfriend, and there was a genuine nervousness building in my gut.

I danced and hung out with other boys who invited me to do so, but would always tell them I wasn't allowed to be alone with a boy if they had the courage to suggest an official date. A few boys in my class did ask, and they were promptly shut down. I was proud of my hard-to-get status.

I was finally sixteen, allowed to date and eager to experience my first passionate kiss. Ethan's full lips looked like they were worthy of the wait. On the days leading up to the dance, I made a point of giving Ethan a few lingering glances when we passed each other in the hall. I was casually laying the groundwork before taking the leap.

When the night finally came, my stomach was churning with doubts and insecurities. I went from being certain he'd say yes to worrying over the possibility that he could say no. I had never made the first move, and Ethan had not said anything to me in so long.

I needed encouragement to follow through with my plan. I invited one of my closest friends, Rachel, to come over prior to the dance, so we could get ready together and masterfully put together an outfit Ethan couldn't possibly resist.

"I was thinking I'd wear my skinny jeans and this top. It shows just a little skin without being obvious." I held up my favorite pair of dark denim jeans and a black, off-the-shoulder, slinky sweater.

"Katelyn, you know you look amazing in anything! You've got nothing to worry about. Every guy in the school will be tripping all over you," Rachel gushed. She knew fully well that the same was true of her, but I felt the need to remind her. We were always building each other up.

"Rachel, you've had almost every guy in school ask you out already! I know we're hotties! I'm sure my confidence will kick in once I'm in the moment. I've only had a few real conversations with him. It's hard to predict his reaction."

"He'll say yes! Now, let's go. We're already more than fashionably late," Rachel urged as she gathered her makeup back into her slick black purse.

My older sister dropped us off at the dance, so we wouldn't be seen with our parents. I had a road test for my learner's permit the next week, and Rachel was still two months away from turning sixteen. Amy was at Windsor University studying engineering and didn't mind driving us since it gave her an excuse to take a break from her studying. She was such an awesome sister.

I shouldn't say *was*, as if she's no longer alive. She's actually doing wonderfully. She's now engaged to a great guy, and working as an engineer at a manufacturing plant in Windsor. I barely saw her during the two years I was away from home; when I finally came back, she had already moved in with Michael. I'm truly grateful to have my sisters back in my life again. I wonder if we would have lost so much time together, if that dance had ended differently.

Thanks to Rachel pumping me up, I strutted into the school gym feeling extra irresistible. My plan was to wait at least a few songs before approaching Ethan. I stood in a circle with my friends and listened as they either raved about or harshly critiqued what everyone else was wearing.

Ethan arrived about ten minutes later. It was already 9:30 p.m., and the dance only lasted until 10:30. Although it technically started at 8:00 p.m., the popular crowd never showed up until at least an hour later.

Within a few minutes of his arrival, I noticed Ethan chatting with a redhead named Cindy, whom I knew from art classes. I watched as both of them laughed and smiled before casually parting ways. I was aware that Ethan had other admirers; I knew I needed to make my move soon. Plus, other boys had worked up the courage to ask my friends to dance. I figured someone would ask me before long, and I only wanted to dance with Ethan.

I gave Rachel's hand a gentle squeeze. She squeezed mine back reassuringly before quickly letting go. At the same time, she was being playfully dragged onto the floor by our good friend Chris. I couldn't stand being alone waiting and wondering anymore.

I exhaled and walked slowly toward Ethan, bracing myself to be brave. He was leaning up against the wall, surrounded by his loyal friends and followers. I broke my way into their circle and looked him straight in the eye.

"I was standing over there with this urge to dance and was thinking you could join me." I practiced the line all day and it sounded as slick and enticing as I had imagined.

"Yeah, I don't really dance." Ethan's eyes met mine.

His cool words were a shock to my gut, but I thought I recovered quite quickly.

"You won't make an exception for me?" My question was accompanied by a bat of the eyes and pout of the lips in a more-adorable-than-cheesy way that I had repeatedly practiced in my bedroom mirror.

"What makes you so exceptional?" Ethan cocked his eyebrow and smirked. A couple of the guys around him giggled childishly.

"Pretty sure most of the guys here would think I'm exceptional! I guess you'll miss out on finding out why. Anyone else interested in that offer?" I replied, trying to sound significantly more confident than I was beginning to feel inside. My eyes connected with my friend Matt, who I thought had a secret crush on me. Matt turned his head to avoid eye contact.

Guys were always asking me out, so I thought it was a safe bet to double down on my desirability. To my utter humiliation and near mortification, the other boys' eyes fell to the floor or darted toward Ethan. Not even the prepubescent, girl-crazed geeks jumped at my open invite to dance. After what felt like forever, I slinked away back to my dwindling group of friends without saying another word. This was the first time that I felt the sting of rejection.

I know most kids experience teasing and various forms of bullying at some point or another through school, but I hadn't. I had sweet, innocent friends in my rural grade school, kids who had known each other since we were in diapers. The only kids who ever got picked on were the unlucky new kids who didn't try to graciously blend in.

I was the new kid in my last year of elementary school, which would normally be at least a difficult adjustment, if not a social disaster. I grew up in a small, middle-class town called Harrow in Southern Ontario. My father's business was continuously expanding, so my parents made the decision to significantly upgrade our quaint little home. We moved fifteen minutes away to the more affluent town of LaSalle.

Making new friends was a lot easier when I was secure in myself. I understood how to fit in with the cool crowd. I was quiet and somewhat shy the first few days at my new school, until I got the chance to learn more about my classmates and the social dynamics. I made sure not to ruffle any feathers and was nice to everyone.

I immediately felt a connection with Rachel. She was beautiful, smart and envied by both girls and guys. I opened the door to a friendship with a little flattery, and we hit it off instantly. My newfound friendship with one of the hottest girls in school, combined with how lustful teenage boys are always chasing the new girl in class, made it easy. I was shielded from the usual bullying and judgment that beats on the self-esteem of the average teenager.

Up until that humiliating moment at that dance when I was sixteen, I never questioned my worthiness or worried whether or not I was accepted.

I may not have made it to everyone's party, but I was always invited. I was not a social outcast. I was a hottie, right?

Or was I?

My mind was rapidly trying to rationalize my exceptional self-confidence. I stood frozen on the gym floor, internally dissecting every aspect of my self-worth. I couldn't find justification for being so rudely rejected. Why was I suddenly being dissed by a large group of boys, including the one exception that I actually thought was worthy of being my first real date?

While I self-consciously slinked back into the small group of girls who weren't already dancing with someone, I could hear Ethan and his minions laughing. For the first time in my life, I had an overwhelming feeling that I was the inspiration for their joke.

Within a few minutes, Rachel realized I wasn't dancing with my crush and excused herself from Chris to make sure I was okay. She sacrificed her romance for me! We snuck outside until Amy came back to pick us up, so that no one else would see me feeling sorry for myself. I was always smiling at school, but I was fighting back the urge to break down in snotty tears after Ethan's dismissal.

Rachel insisted that it was just Ethan being an asshole, and told me I was still pretty. "There is no way that your hot body and gorgeous face suddenly became easily resistible. That's just not possible, Katelyn."

She teased that my boldly asking him out might have been seen as an attack on his manliness. The other boys must have been too intimidated by the situation to react, or they didn't want to cross Ethan. Between my previously solid self-esteem and Rachel's reassurance, I felt certain it was Ethan's issue by the time I fell asleep that evening.

I was the pretty one. Ethan was a foolish boy who would regret his decision.

For someone who didn't suffer from typical teenage insecurities, my impenetrable confidence didn't last very long. Despite our initial impression of the incident at the dance, it wasn't just Ethan who had decided that I was undesirable. It became undeniably obvious that every boy in school was avoiding eye contact with me.

I always viewed Matt as being a close friend. We hung out since grade nine and talked all the time. Now he appeared to be rushing off in the opposite direction whenever I would look his way. Cody used to constantly flirt with me, since our lockers were located side by side. Now, he acted like I didn't exist when we'd bump into each other between periods.

None of the boys in my class were showing *any* interest in me. I was suddenly shunned, and didn't know why. There were even a few moments when it looked like a group of guys were laughing and pointing at me in the hallway between classes. Anytime I witnessed that behavior prior to that dance, I didn't jump to the conclusion that I was the intended target. This time I did.

I couldn't figure out what made me so repulsive and ridiculed, which bothered me more than the fact that I was suddenly the butt of their immature jokes. I tried to keep my mind off Ethan's rejection and my sudden loss in social status, which wasn't easy—even for me.

I was successful for a few weeks, at least until I literally bumped into Ethan between classes. I was rushing out of my first period math class because I had to swing by my locker, on the second floor, and make it back to art class, on the first floor, in less than fifteen minutes. I'd forgotten to bring my tote bag with my art supplies. I was rounding the corner at the top of the stairs when we collided pretty hard.

Ethan was with a few of his buddies, and didn't have the decency to apologize. He didn't even offer to help me pick up the textbooks and pencils that the collision had sent flying down the hall. He shook off the impact and kept moving, as if I was an inanimate object rather than a human being.

How on earth could I have fallen for someone so self-absorbed?

How could I be so invisible to a teenage boy?

I was supposed to be irresistible! Instead of thinking something was wrong with Ethan, my mind switched to obsessing over my looks. Although my body was tight and toned by even the highest standards, I stopped seeing its appeal. I focused too much attention on every minor flaw instead. I started working out obsessively and eating a strict diet of only vegetables and lean protein.

Several weeks after the dance, not one of the guys in my school had even moderately flirted with me. After repeatedly whining to Rachel that I must not be the hottie I thought, she decided to get answers from Chris. He could ask his friends what they thought of me, which would hopefully combat my newfound insecurities.

Chris reluctantly agreed. He couldn't say no to Rachel, as it was becoming quite apparent that they shared the same passionate connection that I used to want with Ethan. A few days later, she came over to my house after school with the scoop. I could tell by her face that it wasn't good news.

"Let me have it, Rachel. I'm ready." I slightly bent my knees and put my hands on my hips as if to brace myself for the physical impact of her words.

"Are you sure you want to know the answer, Katelyn? It's not what you're thinking, but it's not great either," Rachel warned.

"Just tell me. Is it my tiny tits? I wish they were bigger, but is that really all guys care about?"

"It's not your boobs or your body."

"My face?" Which made no sense to me, even as I said it. (This was before the fire, when I still had smooth, evenly-toned skin and two matching ears.)

"No, it's your attitude." My blunt friend replied.

"*What?!*" I answered with more attitude than I intended.

I begun pacing the room while we discussed the results of Chris' male student body survey; and the bomb Rachel dropped had literally stopped me in my tracks. Rachel gave me a sympathetic look and a supportive smile before continuing.

"You're very confident, and they think you're out of their league." I could tell she was trying to downplay their real comments.

"That doesn't make sense. You're definitely out of their league, and they still throw themselves at you. Plus, why would he reject me when I made the first move? Why would I be completely ignored by all these guys?" I argued, my heart racing furiously in my chest.

"They think that you think you're too good for them, and they don't stand a chance." She was trying to explain it so delicately, so as to not further damage my self-esteem. Her efforts were futile.

"So they think I'm a stuck-up snob?" I knew the real meaning behind her words.

"At least it's something you can fix. They just think you're too confident. You've shot down a lot of guys. Chris said Ethan thinks you act like you're better than everyone else, which of course we both know is true. You just need to hide it better." Rachel's pep talk was followed with a wink and a long hug.

Rachel's wise words didn't sink in right away. I stewed over the assessment for a few days, before finally confronting Matt. I wanted to explain to Ethan that he was wrong about me, but I decided that Matt wouldn't be as brutally honest as Ethan. Unfortunately, I was really wrong.

"Can we talk for a moment, Matt?" I cut him off on his way out of school on a Friday. I purposely picked a Friday, so I'd have the weekend to get over it if the response was bad.

"I guess. What about?" Matt tone reeked of annoyance, which was quite out of character.

"Are we friends?" I asked with the utmost sincerity.

"What do you think?" Matt said, raising his left eyebrow.

"I thought we were friends, then something changed. I don't know what I did wrong." My emotions were more fragile than I realized and my lower lip began to quiver.

"What changed is you asking Ethan to dance. We were always hanging out, I was so nice to you and I thought that we would end up dating once you were finally allowed. Apparently, I'm not good enough for you." The reflection in his eyes was clouded by angry tears.

"I didn't think of you that way. I didn't know you liked me that way." I fumbled to reply. Truthfully, I'd thought he had a crush on me, but he never actually said anything to me.

"Bullshit!" He snapped while pushing back the tears that betrayed his emotions. "I was so good to you, and you showed no interest in me. So I stopped wasting my time."

Matt's words dripped with bitterness; his cold stare felt like daggers. I was focused on fighting off the tears threatening to form in my eyes when he stormed away, leaving me puzzled and embarrassed.

Matt had a reputation for being a sweet, soft-spoken guy. That was the first time I had ever seen him angry at anyone, and I felt shame that it was caused by my behavior. I had never had any idea that our friendship hinged on its potential to blossom into a romantic relationship. I was beginning to realize that although I had a right to be fussy over who I chose to be with, the guys I rejected or ignored along the way would not graciously accept defeat.

It took me several weeks, but eventually my self-esteem rebounded—for the most part. I chose to believe that guys being intimidated by me was significantly better than if they thought I was physically undesirable. I made a conscientious effort to be friendlier and actively practiced being humble, hoping it would soften my reputation.

Looking Forward

I refused to let silly boys and their insecurities dictate my future. I knew my potential, and felt certain my life would only get better. Although no one asked me out throughout the remainder of high school (and I did not have the guts to risk humiliation again by making the first move), I was at least able to rebuild close relationships with male friends at my school.

I think that I successfully changed most people's opinion over my attitude by the time we graduated. Being rejected showed me that I was not better than anyone else; I just hoped my new perspective was apparent to the rest of my classmates.

Deep down, I realized that it didn't matter what they thought of me. I was planning on leaving my small-town troubles the following September. Since I was the only one of my friends who didn't spend my senior year attached to a boy, I had plenty of time to map out the life I wanted. My goal was to have a fabulous life that made Ethan wish he had accepted my generous offer to dance.

At first, I thought I could be either a famous model or try to make it as an artist, but the realist in me knew the unlikelihood of any real success. I didn't have the drive or commitment for the Olympics in cross country, even though it was something I was looking forward to attempting at the university level.

My parents encouraged me to go into teaching, since I was patient and well-rounded. Although my guidance counselor agreed that teaching suited my personality and academic performance, she warned me that the job market was headed toward a worrisome decline. My ultimate goal would be to teach art or design, and it was considerably harder to find an artistic teaching position in Ontario.

I spent a lot of time weighing my options before deciding to combine my love of fashion and modeling with my artistic skills. I applied for a variety of fashion and design programs in Ontario, as far away from home as possible. I was genuinely giddy when I found out I was accepted into the Fashion Design program at Ryerson University. It was four hours away, which would give me another fresh start. This time I would make sure my alluring outside was matched with a welcoming personality.

I relished the thought of reinventing myself in a new city. I still felt like I was beautiful and worthy of an exceptional man. University would be my chance to meet a mature man who would recognize my value.

I ended up earning a partial grant and athletic scholarship for track and field. Fortunately, I also received more money than I was expecting from both my parents and grandparents. My father didn't want me working a lot of hours in Toronto, because he feared I'd lose focus on my studies. I started searching for jobs weeks before my first semester started and landed a server position at a cafe close to the campus, working ten to twelve hours a week.

I'm a planner with a positive attitude. Well, I was back then—and I'm trying to be again. I was beyond excited to be going away to university, and took every precaution to ensure it was a successful transition.

I felt slightly bad for my parents, who seemed a tad hurt by how anxious I was to escape our small hometown for big city life in Toronto. It wasn't that I was eager to escape my parents; I was looking forward to being the hot new girl on campus, and finally going on an actual *date*. I would be completely embarrassed if anyone in university discovered that I was the undateable snob from Villanova High School. If asked, I planned on lying and saying I'd been on several dates, but hadn't met the right one.

In university, I made a conscientious effort to not act overly confident or dismissive of men, so no one would mistake my selectiveness for being stuck-up. I attempted to boldly leap into the large social circle the first weekend of school, but it ended up being a far worse experience than the dreaded dance with Ethan two years prior.

Within the first couple of days of school, everyone was talking about a big freshman party being hosted at a house a few blocks from my dorm. The big freshman bash was a yearly tradition, and every new student was invited.

Two different women that I had talked with a few times after class mentioned it to me and said that they were going. My university-assigned roommate, Kassie—whom I clicked with right away—was also planning on checking it out. I was definitely intrigued and figured it was the ideal opportunity to make some new friends, as well as check out the available men. I was eager to establish myself as an easygoing, fun person to know.

It was a warm September evening, so I wore a royal blue, sleeveless summer dress with strappy, low-heeled sandals. Kassie had on a much shorter spandex dress with heels that made me cringe. She, however, walked in them as gracefully as if they were slippers.

The sun was still out when we left, and we bumped into several other classmates headed in the same direction. After about a twenty-minute walk, we finally arrived—and I was caught off guard by the chaos unfolding in front of me. The house was so tightly packed that various teenagers and slightly older students were spread across the entire lawn in smaller cliques.

Although The Tragically Hip was blaring loudly from speakers inside the house, it could barely be heard over everyone screaming as they tried to talk to one another. Almost everyone had a red plastic cup of beer and/or a cigarette dangling from their mouth. I had expected to see alcohol and smoking, just not quite so many people.

Kassie squeezed her way through the crowded entrance, pressing herself up against every guy she passed by. I waited for people to move around enough that I could sneak by without attracting any unwanted attention. I slowly wiggled my way inside the house, searching desperately for an open space to stand. I lost Kassie within the first five minutes, and didn't see her again for the rest of the night. I also never saw any of my other classmates who had originally invited me.

After about fifteen minutes I found the kitchen, which wasn't nearly as crowded. They had two kegs out and booze everywhere. Everyone was helping themselves, so I grabbed an empty cup from the stack and pumped myself a beer. I didn't know that I was supposed to tilt the cup, so of course it overflowed with foam, and the excess made my hands disgustingly sticky.

I noticed a fairly cute, well-dressed man was watching me as I quickly washed my hands in the sink. There was no soap in sight, but the water helped rinse away most of it. As I was drying my hands with a cheap paper towel, he made his way toward me.

"Pouring from a keg is tricky. I'll help you with your next beer."

"Thanks! I didn't realize it would foam over so much," I sheepishly responded. Instinctually, I found myself staring at his feet, too self-conscious to look him in the eyes.

"It'll do that if you don't tilt the cup as it fills." He tilted his head to grab my attention; our eyes met, and we greeted each other with a sincere smile.

I shook off my insecurities and gleefully replied, "Good to know! I barely have any beer hiding under this foam, so I'll be pouring another one soon."

"It's okay. I'll take care of you." The suggestive look he gave me made me tingle inside.

I'm not sure if he was bumped from behind or lost his balance, but he suddenly lurched within inches of my face. His left hand grabbed my right wrist for support. I could smell the beer on his breath.

"You have beautiful eyes," he whispered.

"Um, thank you," I said, turning my head to one side. I'd taken a sip of beer when it was foaming over, and I wasn't sure if my breath was just as rancid as his. He was standing too close and it made me self-conscious. We weren't alone in the kitchen, but he had enough room to take a step back.

"What's your name?" he asked.

"Katelyn. What's yours?" I turned my head to answer, so my beer breath didn't turn him off.

"I am Phil, and I'm going to kiss you," he announced proudly.

With practically no warning, Phil grabbed me, pulled me to him, and started kissing me aggressively. His tongue forced its way into my mouth. I wanted to gag from the smell of churning alcohol. He was squeezing my ass with one hand and trying to stick the other up the front of my dress. I held my legs tightly together in protest.

As I already mentioned, we were far from being alone. I wedged my arm in between us and pushed him away, ending the unwanted kiss. I shook my head in disbelief, disgusted that this virtually average-looking guy thought he could try that with me.

"Oh, come on, it's just a kiss," he arrogantly protested.

"One I didn't ask for, or want," I replied with a fair amount of assertion in my voice. It wasn't the first time I'd had to shoot down a guy's unwanted kiss. However, I was able to deflect the others prior to our lips actually connecting.

What Phil couldn't have possibly guessed was that it was my first real kiss. A boy kissed me on the lips quickly when I was in grade six, but I don't think that truly counts. Other than that innocent peck, I had never let anyone else get that close to me.

None of the partiers surrounding us paid any attention to our uncomfortable encounter. Upon being rejected, Phil sulked off into the front room, and I stood there with a beer shaking in my right hand.

It took me several minutes to snap out of it. I angrily downed the beer and forced my way back through the crowd. I searched the house for about twenty minutes, avoiding the direction Phil went in, but I didn't come across any of my new friends. It was so crowded, you couldn't even see everyone who was in the same room as you.

Eventually, I left the house party by myself. I then made my way home in the dark, alone and pissed off at all mankind. In just the short walk home, I had two different guys shout suggestive remarks at me as they walked past me, and one car honked before another hung halfway out the window yelling, "Strut it, honey!" I was clenching my jaw so tight that it gave me an instant headache.

All men think about is sex!

That thought kept running through my head. Why was I so anxious to get into a relationship, when the guy's sole motivation is getting laid? It wasn't even 9:00 p.m. when I got back to my room, but I was so exhausted and frustrated that I immediately went to bed. I stewed over the stupidity of men, while tossing and turning for at least hour before giving into my pillow.

The next few weeks of university were a socially awkward blur. It was difficult and chaotic adjusting to the demands of my school schedule accompanied by my part-time job, taking care of my own cooking, cleaning, and laundry, as well as finding time to work on my craft or go for a run. Describing it as overwhelming would be an understatement.

I was used to running for at least an hour, five days per week. Now I was lucky if I found the time to train for cross country for an hour each week. There was a sincere fear I wouldn't make the cut and would lose the potential scholarship funds for my second year. At least the busyness of my schedule kept my mind off of the more-than-uncomfortable experience from the one and only university party I attended as a single woman.

Making friends or finding the love of my life dropped to the bottom of my priority list, along with all forms of social interaction. It wasn't until the weekend before Thanksgiving that I had a conversation with my dorm-mate longer than a sentence each. I had just gotten back from a Sunday morning shift at the cafe and was planning on spending the rest of the day finishing a few layouts for a design assignment. We were creating elaborate evening gowns that showcased our imagination, while staying true to our individual style.

I had drawn three different versions and wasn't particularly in love with any of them. They were beautiful, yet lacking in the creativity and innovation I suspected the teacher wanted. Although I appreciate high fashion, my style leaned more toward simplicity and elegance. As I was pulling the designs out of my portfolio case, Kassie interrupted me.

"Katelyn, are you going home for Thanksgiving?"

"Yep. I'm leaving Friday afternoon, and I'll be back Monday night."

"Me too. You're in Windsor, right?" She was staring with a pensive interest.

"LaSalle actually, but I get off the train in Windsor."

"Did you get your train ticket already?" Kassie's expression hinted that she had an alternative plan, but she was taking the long way to get there.

"Yeah, my dad sent them to me last week. Why?" I asked.

"This guy Dave offered me a ride to London, but I'm too nervous to go by myself. He's going with his friend Nathan, and I'll be outnumbered. They're both headed to Windsor afterwards, which is why I thought of you," Kassie explained.

"So, I'd be alone with them from London to Windsor? How's that safe for me?" I replied.

"They're harmless guys from school. Don't be so paranoid, Katelyn!" she insisted.

"You don't want to be alone with them," I argued.

"I'll be with you all the way to London. Just come with me, please," Kassie begged.

"How well do you know these guys? Are they both from Windsor?" The responsible side of me pushed my inquiry further.

"Yes, both good ol' Windsor boys. I met them both a few weeks ago, and I've hung out with them plenty already. I really like Dave. That's where I've been crashing the last few nights. They have an apartment off campus. I've slept there, and came back here alive. I just want female company for the car ride. Please." Kassie was giving it all she could to reassure me.

"I don't know..." My stance started to waiver. Her pouty face made it hard to crush her hopes.

"You can get your money back for the train ticket. Did I mention Nathan is single and sexy as hell? You're single, right? You need some fun. Let's do this!" Kassie pleaded enthusiastically.

"Yeah, sure. That could work," I said hesitantly, while I continued to debate the idea in my head.

I wasn't looking forward to the five-hour train ride; we'd most likely get there faster by car, even stopping in London. The last few weeks were filled with only school, work, and running, which left no time to engage with other people. I was craving human contact. Plus, I was anxious to see if I was desirable again. A car ride with a cute single guy could be exactly what I need to recharge my self-esteem. I was slowly nodding along as I rationalized it in my head.

"Yes! So, you'll come with me? I'll owe you one," Kassie wheedled.

"All right, it sounds like a great idea. I'll go—as long as I can get a refund for my dad on the ticket. What time are we leaving?"

"I think he said we'd leave Friday sometime before lunch, but I'll get the full details from Dave tonight. I'm going over there to watch a movie after I'm done studying. Do you want to come too? His roommate's probably home." She stretched the last few words into almost a song, trying to tempt me into joining her.

"I'm a mess, and I need to tweak my design layouts—plus I still have a lot of studying to do. I'll meet him Friday." She couldn't persuade me again.

"Totally get it! Thanks again for agreeing to go."

Kassie grabbed a Dr. Pepper from the fridge and began to pace the room while reading her psychology notes. She held her typed notes in her left hand, inches from her face, while taking slow carefully sips from the can in her right hand.

"You're going to either spill that on yourself or walk into a wall," I teased.

"I need to cram as much of this as I can into my brain tonight before my test tomorrow. If I sit down to read, I'll crash." She sounded out of breath, as if she had just finished a tough workout.

Kassie studied while pacing the dorm for about ten minutes before tossing her notes onto her bed and rushing to Dave's apartment. I couldn't imagine being so interested in a guy that I would brush off my studying. I had big goals for myself when I first started university, and being a lovestruck fool simply wasn't one of them. If only I had been able to maintain that perspective, I would have saved myself so much emotional and physical pain.

First Impressions

On the following Friday, Dave and Nathan were supposed to pick us up at 10:30 a.m., at the entrance on the far east side of the university parking lot. The plan was to grab lunch at the first rest stop outside of Toronto, and make it home in time for dinner. My mom was splurging on seafood and steaks to celebrate my visit. She scheduled it for 6:00 p.m., because even with lunch and holiday traffic, it shouldn't take us more than five hours to get home.

There was a brief time when I forgot how lucky I am to be a part of this family, but they are the best! Even though my mother was already making a huge Thanksgiving dinner, she insisted on hosting another fancy dinner to welcome me home. My parents would do anything for their daughters.

Kassie and I grabbed the stuff we were bringing home and headed outside around 10:15 a.m. She didn't want Dave waiting for us. We arrived at the meeting spot with several minutes to spare, but he was definitely not as punctual. In fact, we stood there waiting until well after 11:00 a.m. My frustration increased with every minute, until I finally burst.

"Call him, Kassie! He's a half hour late and I want to get home before dinner!" I loudly snapped at her.

"I'll text him." Kassie stared at her phone, nervously, trying to decide what to type. "I don't want to come off high maintenance or demanding. He is the one giving us a ride."

"He should have enough respect to tell you that he's running behind. It's not like he's only a few minutes late." I turned to look the other way because I knew an instinctual eye roll was imminent.

"Fine. I'll just ask if he's on his way." Kassie fingernails slowly clicked against her phone. I watched her pause and read it to herself before finally hitting send. A few minutes of me pacing and panicking passed before he responded.

"It's okay. He says he's on his way," she tried to reassure me.

I nodded politely, but my jaw was clenched so tight it hurt. I calmed myself down by calculating that there was still enough time for us to stop for lunch, drop off Kassie in London, and make it home for dinner. However, after another twenty minutes of impatiently waiting, the odds of making it home in time were slipping away.

"Kassie, they are now an hour late. This is ridiculous. I need to find a way home."

"Give it fifteen more minutes, please. I'm sure they're on their way and have a good excuse." There was her pouty face again, chipping away at my anger with her.

They did arrive within the next ten minutes—but their excuse was inexcusable. They drank too much the night before, woke up hungover, and decided to hit a breakfast buffet. They needed grease to calm their stomachs.

How on earth could they think that's a good enough reason to keep two women waiting for over an hour? We should have at least been invited to join them for breakfast, as a replacement for our original lunch plans. Our road trip was not off to an impressive start.

However, I was so relieved that our ride had finally arrived that I let the bitterness subside quite quickly. Both guys got out of the car and helped us load our luggage. Dave apologized for being late, and Nathan quietly nodded in agreement. Nathan also offered the front seat to Kassie, which I thought showed a little old-fashioned charm.

Nathan was as attractive as Kassie had alluded. He had wavy, dark brown hair that flowed effortlessly to his chiseled chin. His eyes had both the Brad Pitt instant arousal effect and the James Bond intriguing-man-of-mystery appeal. He was dressed casually in dark denim and a maroon T-shirt, which had a subtle logo I didn't recognize on the left side of his chest.

Nathan spent the first half of the car ride asking questions about me. Dave and Kassie were flirting and singing songs together in the front seat, while Nathan enquired about my family, schooling, hobbies and future plans. I had never met a man who was so focused on getting to know me. Conversation flowed uninterrupted.

I was intentionally trying to sound less confident than normal. The harsh lesson Ethan taught me in high school kept running through my mind. I humbly accepted his compliments on my appearance, and down-played my personal achievements. I made a point of asking him all the same questions and paying close attention to his answers.

Nathan was an only child who grew up in South Windsor. On the car ride, he told me his father owned a machine shop and his mother was a librarian. He didn't tell me until a few weeks later that his dad had died when he was in eighth grade. I remember thinking back on our original discussion and wondering why I didn't notice any sense of loss or sadness in his voice when he first mentioned his father.

After about two hours of driving, my stomach started to noticeably growl. I had only eaten a small orange since I woke up. I was expecting that we would have stopped for lunch by now, since we had already been on the road for over an hour. Fortunately (and unfortunately), Nathan heard it too.

"Are you hungry?" he asked with big, sympathetic puppy eyes.

"Guess it's pretty obvious. Are we still planning on stopping for lunch at some point?" I asked timidly. "Kassie implied we would stop, and I haven't eaten much today."

"Dave," Nathan called to him from the backseat. "These ladies need lunch. We were supposed to stop for lunch."

"Oh, shit! You hungry, doll?" Dave turns to Kassie and gives her an exaggerated pout.

"I could eat, if you don't mind." Kassie responded in an overly-cute baby doll voice.

"All right, we'll stop at the next exit," Dave agreed.

It turned out the next exit was London, so we stopped at the first McDonald's. Kassie, who knew she was within minutes of being home, ordered a side salad and diet pop. I was still almost two hours away from being home, and needed to calm the noisy beast in my belly. I ordered a chicken sandwich with fries. I rarely eat fast food, and surprisingly it tasted much better than I remembered. Even though the guys had stuffed themselves at a buffet, they ordered and inhaled a large fry and a ten pack of chicken nuggets each.

When we went to drop Kassie off, it turned into a twenty-minute goodbye kiss at her house. It was followed by a five-minute debate over where we should sit for the rest of the ride. Nathan didn't want to leave me in the back by myself, Dave didn't want to drive in the front by himself, and I was reluctant to sit up front with Dave, considering he was my roommate's boyfriend.

Nathan finally volunteered to give Dave a break from driving, so we could ride in the front together. The next hour or so was spent laughing and singing along to the radio, while Dave napped in the backseat. Dave didn't wake up until we saw the Tilbury sign, thirty minutes from home.

"Are we almost there? I need to piss!" Dave hollered from the back after shaking the sleep from his face.

"Yeah, not far. I'm dropping Kassie off in LaSalle first," Nate called back to him.

"No, I need to get home. Come on, it's my car. We're not driving all the way to LaSalle. Go to my house, and she can take a cab from there." Dave's earlier charm had disappeared, now that Kassie was no longer in earshot.

"That's fine," I muttered, trying to avoid this dispute. I knew my father would pick me up if I asked him.

"No, I'll drive you home after I drop off Dave. Can I borrow your car for twenty minutes once you're home?" Nathan suggested as a compromise.

"Sure, whatever. I just want to get home. My stomach is still jacked from last night. I shouldn't have had more crap at McDonalds," Dave whined.

I thanked both of them and we made arrangements to meet up again on Monday at 10:30 a.m. We exchanged phone numbers in case anyone was going to be late (again). I was going to get my sister Amy to drop me off at Dave's, and we'd leave from his house. We dropped off Dave and proceeded to drive the short distance to my parents.

"Thanks for borrowing his car. I'm sure you're anxious to get home too," I said as he pulled into our two-car driveway.

"Not really. You were a great travel companion. I'm looking forward to the ride home already." He was staring at me in a way that caused me to blush.

"You too," I mumbled in a tone that was almost barely audible, before turning to let myself out. Nathan immediately followed, and retrieved my bag from the trunk. He walked it to my front door before giving me an innocent wave goodbye.

I turned around in the driveway to flash Nathan a flirtatious smile before he had a chance to get back inside Dave's car. This was a man worthy of my time. Dinner was practically on the table when I walked inside, but I didn't regret my decision to not take the train. I was already looking forward to the ride home in three days.

Luckily for me, I didn't have to wait until the ride home to hear from Nathan. He sent me a text Saturday afternoon, asking me if I was busy the entire weekend. I had plans with Rachel that evening, but we could easily switch it to a double date. Rachel had recently moved into apartment near the University of Windsor with her boyfriend Chris, and she was excited to show it to me.

Unfortunately, Nathan didn't go for the suggestion, saying that he would rather get to know me one-on-one first. He confessed that he'd be nervous meeting my best friend so soon, and his logic made sense to me. Instead, he offered to take me for dinner; then he would drop me off at Rachel's afterwards. He didn't have a car, so he borrowed Dave's again. I told my mom about bailing on our family dinner and she was super supportive.

"Don't worry about it. We had that lovely dinner last night, and the entire family is coming here tomorrow for Thanksgiving. Go, enjoy yourself. Maybe it'll work out and you'll be bringing him to Christmas dinner." My mom reassured me she understood.

(I assume she's always wondered why she never sees me going on dates or talking about potential boyfriends. She probably thinks I've kept stuff like that from her because I'm not overly forthcoming with any personal details of my life. I doubt she realizes that I had no dates to speak of, not fondly or otherwise.)

I spent the next two hours fussing over what I should wear. I called Rachel, and she told me not to worry if I showed up late or needed to postpone. As excited as we were to see each other, she was the only other person who truly knew that this was my very first official date.

Nathan picked me up at 5:30 p.m., just as promised. He suggested the local high-end steakhouse, The Keg, which was too good to pass up. He laughed at me teasingly when I ended up ordering chicken.

"You're not supposed to order chicken at the Keg. That's sacrilegious." He was trying to sound serious, but couldn't help but crack a smile.

"They make great chicken here, too; otherwise it wouldn't be on the menu," I playfully pleaded my case.

"If you don't like steak, we could have gone somewhere else."

"I love steak, but I had it for dinner last night," I explained.

"We still could have gone somewhere else. Why didn't you say anything?" His tone was sounding more sincere by the second.

"The chicken sounds amazing, and I love the atmosphere here. I was excited you suggested this place," I said with the utmost sincerity.

"Good," Nathan replied with a firm confidence.

I was thrilled that my first official date was at a high-class, romantic restaurant rather than a fast food joint. I wanted it to be memorable, and this certainly met all of the requirements. Everything from the food to the conversation left me wanting more. He didn't even try to kiss me goodnight when he dropped me off. This was how I imagined dating should be.

It was going so well that I wanted to extend the date beyond dinner, but I insisted on sticking with my plans—mostly because I was dying to tell Rachel all about Nathan. I knew starting slow was the smart idea, especially since he was my ride back to university on Monday.

The rest of the weekend flew by, because all I could think of was Nathan. He called me Sunday afternoon to say he had a great time on Saturday and was hoping we could do it again soon. I told him that I was sure we'd figure out a date that worked for both of us, and we could chat more about what to do on the ride back to Toronto. Nathan then offered to pick me up at my parents', instead of making Amy drive me to Dave's.

"I told Dave your house is less than ten minutes out of our way and insisted we would pick you up. It's the gentlemanly thing to do, so expect us around 10:30 a.m. I'll even force him to be on time." The sound of Nathan's stern yet sweet voice gave me a giddy smile that I couldn't shake.

We started the ride back the same way we ended the ride there, with Dave sleeping in the back seat. Fortunately, the guys were only fifteen minutes late this time. I gave my parents and sisters another round of goodbye hugs and hopped in the front seat with Nathan. Dave didn't even stir.

Nathan shot me a wide, smooth smile before turning his attention back to the street. He smelled like Axe body spray and peppermint. We quickly made our way to the main highway in utter silence; he looked deep in thought. I had a hunch he was searching for a clever icebreaker, and I was right.

Out of nowhere he asked, "Did you eat any pizza while you were home?"

"No, did you?" I was puzzled, since he knew I'd had steak Friday, chicken Saturday, and Thanksgiving dinner on Sunday.

"I had some almost every day. I always heard that Windsor was known for having the best pizza, but I didn't fully appreciate why until I tried the pizza place on campus. I've had pizza from four different places in Toronto, and none of them came close to Naples." Nathan's passion for pizza was adorable.

"I've heard that about Windsor pizza, too. I just don't crave pizza that often. I prefer a thick cheeseburger with fries, if I'm going to splurge and eat something sinful."

"I won't turn down a good cheeseburger either. I found a great burger joint about ten minutes from campus. We should go there for dinner one night," he suggested, in a manner as casual as his worn-out jeans and plain navy t-shirt. He was effortlessly attractive.

"Absolutely! I haven't had much time to tour anything off campus. I would love to check out more of the neighborhood," I responded more eagerly than I intended. I was completely lacking my usual cool.

"We can walk there, have a bite together and see what else is around. I'm free Thursday and Saturday night, so far."

"Saturday works for me!" I was grinning like a teenage girl gushing over her boy crush. Fortunately, Nathan's eyes were firmly focused on the road.

"Then it's a date!" From my side view I could see that his grin was almost as wide as mine as we settled on the plans for our second date.

Dave slept until we picked up Kassie. He quickly rubbed his eyes, took a gulp of the cold coffee next to him, and instantly reverted back into Prince Charming. He even managed to get out of the car and open the door for her before she reached the vehicle. The two of them went from flirting to making out in the backstreet in mere seconds, as Nathan and I made comfortable chit chat in the front.

The drive to Toronto seemed faster than ever before because the conversation never ceased. Nathan helped me with my bags and gave me a quick kiss on the cheek before heading back to their car. He even sent a text later, wishing me a good night's sleep. We sent cute messages back and forth all week, and I was giddy by the time Saturday arrived. I changed my outfit six times, spent an hour on my hair, and still didn't feel my usual confidence.

I ended up calling Rachel, because I knew she'd give me the pep talk I desperately needed. She assured me that it was obvious he was interested in me. She told me that I'm pretty and there's no reason why any guy wouldn't be attracted to me. As long as I didn't act overly cocky or self-absorbed, the date would be just as wonderful as the first.

Nathan arrived on time, looking like he belonged on the cover of GQ. We walked slowly side by side, as he pointed out different shops and places he had visited since moving in with Dave. The burger tasted like heaven, but was way too sloppy for me to eat like a lady. Nathan let out a hearty laugh when he noticed I had cheese hanging from my chin, before telling me how much he appreciated a woman with a real appetite.

"I hate when you go on a date and she orders a small salad, insisting she's too full to finish it and then her stomach is rumbling the rest of the night. Eat a real meal and enjoy it!" Every word that trickled from his mouth sounded sexier than it should.

"Truthfully, I do eat fairly healthy most of the time, but that doesn't mean I don't appreciate a thick burger covered in cheese and bacon once in a while."

Conversation came easily with him. Nathan walked me all the way back to my dorm, and we ended the night with a long, sensual kiss. It felt nothing like the sloppy, beer-reeking kiss from the previous episode. There was clear body language that we both wanted more, but I forced myself to pull away. My plan was to wait until I was ready to have sex before telling him that I was still a virgin. I wasn't ready to do either.

"Wow, you're a good kisser. Unfortunately, I need to call it a night." I gave him a quick peck and turned toward the entrance to my building.

"Do you have to go? We could go back to my place?" Nathan tugged on my arm playfully.

"No, I should go. Can we do this again?"

"Yes, and hopefully more..." He pulled me toward him for another lingering kiss.

"You never know," I flirted back.

"I can't convince you to come home with me?" He asked again, batting his thick lashes over sad puppy-dog eyes.

"Not this time. Maybe after our next date," I replied with a sultry pout. I didn't think I would be ready next time either, but I was worried that if I blew him off completely, he might lose all interest.

"I'm sure you're worth the wait," he said with a playful wink, before turning to leave. I was hopeful he'd still feel that way if he struck out again on our next date. And what if I wasn't worth the wait? He assumed that I had plenty of opportunities to practice. I had never even picked up the ball.

I understood the basics, but all the mixed reviews I heard from my friends over the years made me nervous. I was worried I wouldn't enjoy it—or even worse, he wouldn't because I failed to do something right. The success and confidence I had in other areas of my life didn't give me the reassurance I needed to feel certain I'd be a good lover.

Instead of studying on Saturday for a midterm in my intro to business class, I spent the afternoon Googling sex advice and soft porn. I was nineteen, and tired of being the only virgin I knew. I had found a guy who was interested in me, and I was committed to having sex before the offer was taken off the table. My desperation was proof that suddenly going from the hot chick to an undesirable reject in high school had a detrimental affect on my self-esteem, no matter how hard I tried to pretend that it didn't.

Two days later, after a fair amount of sexually-suggestive texting, Nathan invited me over to watch movies at their apartment. Coincidentally, Dave was coming by our dorm room to hang out with Kassie. My stomach started to ache the moment I realized that we would be spending the evening alone within footsteps of Nathan's bedroom.

A lot more preparation goes into getting ready for a date when you think it might be the night you finally lose your virginity. I shaved any unwanted hair I could find, applied lotion on every inch of my body, and put on the sexiest matching bra and thong set I owned. I kept telling myself that I would say yes if the opportunity presented itself.

Nathan didn't suggest going for dinner first or offer to pick me up, which I was somewhat frustrated by. I didn't want him to think of me as a cheap date if he was expecting it to end with sex. However, it seems those chivalrous qualities are rare within my generation. It's the price women pay in exchange for equality.

Infatuation Escalation

I arrived at the guy's apartment in a loose, yet flattering summer dress that stopped just past my knees. I had on flat, strappy sandals and less makeup than usual. I didn't want it to smear and look obvious when things heated up. Physically, I felt ready. Emotionally, I felt numb.

I began reflecting on that feeling and was lost in my thoughts the first fifteen minutes of our date. He was telling me a funny story about a guy in his class and I was nodding along, while internally debating if I should actually make love for the first time with someone I wasn't certain I even loved. This relationship was way too new for me to feel anything real.

Nathan was a charming guy and things were going well, but I didn't know him well enough to decide whether or not love was even possible. I always thought my first time would be with someone special. I was hoping to make love, not just have horny sex.

Apparently, I was so lost inside my head that I missed his last question. I realized he was looking directly at me, awaiting a response. "Sorry, what did you say?" I asked nervously, while he stared at me with a puzzled look on his face.

"What? Hello! Katie, are you with me? I asked what I could get you to drink, listed a bunch of options and you just nodded. Is everything okay?" He looked genuinely concerned.

"Sorry, yes, I got lost in thought for a second. I'd love a drink. Would you mind repeating my choices?" I gave him an oversized smile and batted my eyes innocently.

"As I was saying while you were lost in space, I have beer, vodka, rye, orange juice, Coke, and milk. If it makes it easier, you can help yourself." His charming tone faded a bit as he pointed toward their small kitchenette.

"Oh sure, yes. I'll make something. What can I get you?"

"I'll have a rye and Coke. Thanks, Love!" he said, while leaning in for a gentle peck on my lips.

Without hesitation, I mindlessly walked to the fridge, searched the cupboards for two clean glasses and made us both a strong mixed drink. As I was preparing our drinks, I tried to rationalize his use of the word love as a sign we would eventually fall in love. I finally gave my head a shake, realizing I needed to get out of my mind and into the moment. Otherwise our date would be a disaster.

I cuddled up to him on the couch, as he flicked through the stations, trying to decide what we should watch. I insisted that it didn't matter to me. It was true, because my mind was too focused on what might happen in real life. After he describe several options, he settled on *The Dark Knight* when he learned that I had never seen it.

Within a few minutes of cuddling, I could feel his right hand inching closer to my trembling thighs. He started off by resting it on the edge of my knee and then subtly readjusted himself, so it was mid-thigh. Now his fingers were starting to dip toward the valley made by my legs coming together. There was an intense tingling sensation throughout my body.

In a flawless swoop, Nathan reached across with his left hand and scooped my right hand up in his. He slowly stroked the top of it, looked deep into my eyes and softly whispered, "You're so beautiful. I feel lucky just being able to touch you." He then leaned in for a long, powerful kiss. It was our best kiss yet.

His hand began exploring my quivering body as we kissed. There was no direct invitation or conversation. His fingers entered me first, as his lips dropped from my mouth to my neck. Once I was ready and wet, he removed his hand long enough to pull my thong down toward my ankles. I didn't fight it. I was ready.

Just as I accepted the reality that this would be my "first time" story, I felt the force of Nathan sliding inside me. Fortunately, the initial discomfort and pain faded as quick as I felt it. I was too focused on trying to wiggle one of my feet out of the thin, silky undies that were currently acting as shackles.

The sex didn't last very long. I was internally debating what position I should suggest we move into when he had an unexpected and explosive orgasm. I couldn't say the same, but was relieved that he was satisfied. Just like that, the virginity I had clung to all of my teenage life was gone in a matter of minutes.

An awkward exchange soon followed, as half-naked Nathan stood up to get a washcloth. He was only wearing a shirt, and his penis bobbed as he walked. It had shrunk to half the size it had felt only moments earlier. He thoroughly cleaned himself and then handed me the soiled cloth. I wiped myself gently with my back turned to him before sliding my stretched underwear back on.

Nothing went the way I thought it would. After we put our clothes back on, he gave me a kiss on the cheek, told me I was great, and returned to watching Heath Ledger embody the legendary Joker within the same breath. His casual response confirmed what I already knew; this was not Nathan's first time.

All I could muster was a meek thank you, as I settled back into the couch. I pretended to stare at the TV while trying to put what happened into perspective. Nathan was a nice guy, I was in university, and meaningless sex is normal. I had spent too many years romanticizing the possibilities, and it left me with impossible expectations.

At least he cared enough to hand me a towel to clean myself. I could tell he liked me, and I was sure the sex would get better once we became more comfortable with each other. We made plans to grab a bite to eat the following day, and called it a night shortly after the movie ended.

He offered to walk me halfway home, but when I said he didn't have to, he let it go without a second offer. He also didn't text me later to make sure I got home safe. These were simple things I expected of my first real love. Nathan was disappointing, but I assumed that was just men today in general. True gentlemen are few and far between.

At least he sent a text first thing the next morning.

Been thinking about you all night. Your body is amazing.

I blushed at the phone and grinned with confidence. I didn't want to come off too eager, so I waited fifteen minutes before texting back.

Yours is pretty impressive too.

Thirty minutes later, he replied.

Busy day, pop by after 9 p.m. if you want.

The day before, we'd talked about grabbing a bite to eat either early afternoon, when we both had a break in our schedule, or at 6:30 p.m. before separating to study for the evening. Suddenly, he's inviting me over for what felt like a booty call. I wasn't sure if he'd forgotten what we discussed or if he was playing games, but I refused to be at his beck and call. I waited over two hours, until it was twenty minutes before my afternoon break.

Grabbing a bite at the cafe in 20 minutes, meet me then. Don't think I'll make it tonight.

I read it over ten times before hitting send. My stomach began turning the moment it was too late to retract. Thoughts of being rejected at my high school dance for my fierce confidence resurfaced. Would Nathan think that I was acting like I was too good for him?

Nathan must have been busy, because he didn't answer until almost 9 p.m.

Heading back to the apartment now. Love to see you there, beautiful.

Every inch of me felt like it would send the wrong message if I went, especially if I ended up having sex with him again—yet my better judgment somehow lost the battle. I paced my apartment trying to decide how to respond, changed my clothes five times and at least made him come to me—but somehow, I talked myself into it. Or more accurately, he talked me into it. It started when I finally replied to his text at 9:30 p.m.

Just saw this now and it's already pretty late.

Three minutes later, Nathan responded.

Not too late for me. I was looking forward to your smile all day.

Two minutes later, I replied.

We should have met for a bite to eat earlier. Maybe tomorrow?

Two minutes later, he sent a lukewarm, useless text:

idk

It felt like I was suddenly getting the brush off, and I wasn't willing to walk away from the relationship so fast. While I was trying to think of how I could entice him into a real date the next day, he sent a second text.

Crammed schedule tomorrow, but want to see you soon. What are you doing now?

So, I caved.

Just studying before bed.

He replied in seconds.

Come here to study, or I'll come there. I can't stop thinking about how sexy you looked last night.

Trying to withhold some of my power, I decided to at least make him come to me.

You can come here, but I need to study.

Studying ceased as soon as I hung up the phone. I changed into baggy yoga pants and a loose tank top, with another tighter tank top underneath. In my head, it wasn't very sexy. In retrospect, maybe it was? Regardless of its simplicity, it worked for Nathan, because he was combing every inch of my body with his eager fingers almost the moment he walked through the door. He kept telling me how irresistible I was, and that he couldn't control himself around me.

Who wouldn't be flattered by that?

He came running to me when I asked, which meant I still had the upper hand. I promised myself that I would maintain control and make better decisions than Kassie did with Dave. We kissed, we groped each other frantically, and eventually, he reached his orgasm. We made a little small talk and then he went home for the night, so I could get back to my studying.

"I know school is important to you, and I want to make sure you have time for your studies. We can get together again later in the week." Nathan gave me a gentlemanly kiss on the cheek before leaving for the night. I was too smitten to study, but at least I still had the option.

Our next few encounters continued in a similar manner, and real feelings of love soon followed. He wasn't clingy or constantly fussing over me, yet he gave me his full attention any time we were together. He made me feel special and desirable.

I balanced my responsibilities and our budding relationship quite well for the first few weeks. I stuck to my daily routine of school and work, only squeezing in a couple nights a week with Nathan after my studying was done. He understood my priorities, and encouraged me to put my schooling ahead of him. I gave up cross country, but only because I was on the cusp of being cut from the team anyway. My fastest wasn't fast enough to compete at the university level, and I didn't have the ambition or time to train enough to improve my speed.

Well, that's at least how our relationship was in the beginning. It wasn't until I was preparing for my exams in the beginning of December that things slowly changed between us. I broke plans with him twice in the same week because I was working on a major runway project. Nathan wasn't pleased.

I sent him a text earlier in the day, explaining that I wasn't able to meet him that evening as we had planned. I was expecting his usual reply: *OK, what about tomorrow?* Instead, he waited a few hours and called me rather than texting. We rarely talk on the phone. After we exchanged normal pleasantries, Nathan let his frustrations be known.

"All right, Kate. I know you want to be a famous designer. I get it. I, however, want a girlfriend who has time for me, and I just don't think you care enough about this relationship to make it work."

His voice was cold and distant, lacking his usual charm. I was in the middle of changing into a pair of yoga pants when he called. I had one leg in, was about to step into the other, when his words forced me into a dead stop. I stood there half-naked, unsure how to respond. Before I could muster up a response, Nathan continued.

"It's nothing against you, Katie-pie. You're just so smoking hot that I get bitter when you break plans. I want you with me; if you don't want the same, I need to find someone who does. I think you deserve the truth." He was direct with his feelings, a quality I had admired since we met.

That was the second time Nathan called me Katie-pie. I used to insist on people using my full name, Katelyn, but I loved the way he made it sound like cutie-pie. I wanted to be with him. I didn't want to be rejected by another guy because I was too stuck on myself to care about his needs.

"I do want to be with you!" I exclaimed loudly into the phone. "I love spending time together, and I promise I'll make more time for us once exams are over."

"I'm not trying to pressure you. I like that you're hardworking and dedicated. It's just not what I want in a girlfriend right now. We're young. I want someone I can make crazy memories with before I settle down," he explained delicately.

"I can be dedicated to you and school. If you give me an hour to make some real progress on my project, maybe we can get together after? You're important to me." I begged him to reconsider.

It was already eight o'clock and I needed to spend at least an hour on my layouts, but I didn't want to lose him. I let go of the waistband to my yoga pants and kicked them off, then I started searching for my tightest pair of jeans instead.

"Will you come here? I went to your dorm the last few times, and you always have to kick me out. Work on your project, then come here after and spend the night," Nathan suggested.

"Sounds like a great idea. I'll be there before ten."

"Show up whenever. I'll be here," Nathan replied emotionlessly.

It was a fair compromise, and definitely better than suddenly calling it quits. I rushed through my sketches, neglecting the intricate details I usually fussed over, feeling certain I'd find time to fix it before submitting it to my professor. I left the dorm within twenty minutes of our conversation ending, and at least five of those minutes were spent making sure I looked irresistible.

Nathan definitely thought so. He gave me a long, sensual kiss before stepping back to get a better look at the tight purple tank top I was wearing with equally tight, slinky, skinny jeans. It was chilly out, so my bare, toned arms were covered by a cropped black puffy jacket.

It didn't take long for Nathan to take it all off. Each time we had sex, it lasted a little longer and he spent a bit more time focused on my needs. This time he kissed every inch of my body first, whispering things like, "I didn't want to let this soft skin go" and "I want to memorize every inch of your body in case this ever ends." His tongue explored me fervently before he came up for air.

"We need to make time for this. This is amazing. I'm addicted to you, and I don't want this to end. I want you," Nathan proclaimed as he thrust himself hard against my body.

His gushing over me made my body quake with anticipation. When he finally entered me, I felt the real power of an orgasm. My toes curled, my back straightened and a piercing groan of approval escaped.

Once I felt the thrill of passionate sex, I wanted it more and more. My relationship with Nathan instantly went from awkward and stale college sex to wild and experimental committed-couple love-making. Falling in love with each other only seemed natural.

Besides school and my part-time job, we spent most of the week together. We ate almost every meal together, I slept at his place most nights, and we filled our spare moments with hardcore sex-capades. I had spent my whole life trying to fill this role of the perfect daughter or potential wife. Being the best student possible and holding the highest of standards had kept me from experiencing the freedom of imperfection. It was oddly empowering.

Reflecting back on the more adventurous sex and how my first real orgasm inspired such a strong addiction, that was only small part of why I put up with so much shit after our romance heated up. It wasn't so much the great sex that had hooked me; he was the first guy who wanted me so badly that he couldn't keep his hands off me. It was flattering and reassuring.

Nathan met my parents at Christmas and charmed them thoroughly. He had my mom laughing so hard that she snorted loudly, causing the rest of us to join in. My older sister, Amy, gave me a squeeze after he went home for the evening and whispered, "I think you've found the one!"

Nathan went with me to visit my grandma in Hamilton on our way home from LaSalle, and even *she* liked him. My dad's mom is a tough old broad who usually complains about everything and everyone. As we were leaving her apartment after visiting for an hour, my grandma gave us her blessing in her usual pushy fashion.

"Katelyn, you have a good man here. Be good to him, so he'll marry you. You're not getting any younger and you should settle down soon, so I can meet my great-grandbabies before the Lord takes me," my always honest Grandma advised us, while clutching her chest dramatically as if her impending demise was imminent.

My embarrassment rose to my cheeks and burned them a bright red, but Nathan didn't run from the pressure. Instead he responded, "I doubt the good Lord is even thinking about taking you. You have a lot of life left in you. Plus, your granddaughter is a pretty smart cookie. I don't think she'll let me go. She knows a good thing when she sees it."

Nathan gave her a soft kiss on the cheek and we headed back to university. I grinned from ear to ear the entire way, because not only did I have an official boyfriend, my whole family liked him as well. Nathan was worth the wait.

We made it back to Toronto on December 30th and decided to part ways for the evening. We already had plans to ring in the New Year at a party with Dave, Kassie, and a huge group of other students.

Nathan surprised me by renting us a room at a hotel within walking distance. We danced and drank a few beers at the party to ring in the New Year before sneaking off to the hotel to ravish each other until the sun came up. Nathan was a bit tipsy, but it didn't spoil our fun.

I loved waking up in his arms.

We were both busy with school and work for most of January, but we made sure to find time for each other. I even switched my days at the café from Tuesday and Thursday nights plus Sunday mornings to only Tuesday and Friday nights. Nathan worked Friday nights as a bartender because the tips were too good to pass on, so it made more sense that I was working the same day. His dad had died when he was thirteen, and he inherited $60,000 from his father's business before he went off to college. He always had cash on him and was quite generous.

Although Nathan had money and would spend it on others, he enjoyed simple pleasures just like me. He bought me a long stem rose and a thick wooly scarf for my birthday on February 2nd. He signed the card, *For my precious flower, love Nathan*. I was head over heels in love with him.

Everything was going better than I expected, up until the end of the school year. It was time for me to prepare for my exams and once again, I couldn't spend as much time with Nathan as he would have liked. We still spoke every day and saw each other a couple times a week, but he was clearly frustrated with our lack of daily love-making by the first week of April.

"I haven't seen you in three days. Why can't you spend the night?" he pleaded at first.

"I need to get up early, and I haven't finished my notes for tomorrow's test. I'll come back tomorrow night for dinner. Plus, we can spend all of Saturday together."

"Just dinner again? Are you going to rush out on me like tonight?" Nathan couldn't hide his disappointment and his sultry-sad eyes were hard to resist. I was infatuated with how much he desired me.

"It's almost summer break, and we'll have more time together then. I need to put school first this time. Please?" I begged.

Nathan sulked, but eventually gave in. He went to the bar instead and must have had a good time, because I didn't hear from him until mid-afternoon the following day. I was able to finish and review my notes, and ended up passing the test with only a few minor mistakes. Both of us were quite busy until school ended, so we only sent the occasional text and didn't make plans together until the weekend we were headed home for the summer.

I decided to spend the night at Nathan's, and then the four of us would drive home whenever we woke in the morning. Kassie was practically living with Dave by that point. Nathan told me that they fought like a married couple, but only when I wasn't around. He couldn't stand the arguing, so he'd often go for a walk to give them space. On the morning we left for home, they gave me the impression of an incredibly happy couple.

Nathan and I, on the other hand, did not. He barely spoke to me during the four-hour ride, and seemed distracted. He wasn't rude or snappy, but he also didn't open the car door for me or offer to stop for breakfast. My stomach was aching for food by the time he dropped me off at my house. However, he did convince Dave to drop me off at my house first.

I got out of Dave's car to grab my luggage from the trunk, but Nathan beat me to it. He handed it to me at the end of the driveway, giving me an opportunity to kiss him goodbye, and asked about our plans for the following night. Originally, we had agreed on the first night home being spent with family and making the second night our date night, but we hadn't decided exactly what we would be doing.

"Let's tackle seeing our families first, and we can figure out the rest tomorrow. I'll text you."

"Sure, okay. Love you!" I eagerly replied.

He just gave me a big smile and got back inside the car. It was early in the afternoon on a Friday and my family wasn't home yet from work. I was tired first from Nathan and I making up for lost time with a passionate evening and another wild round of lovemaking that morning, accompanied by the strain of stressing over our awkward car ride.

I put my bag in my childhood bedroom and crashed between the fluffy pink pillows without stopping in the kitchen for the much-needed snack my stomach was screaming to inhale. I slept until I heard my dad calling for me, shortly after five o'clock.

"It's so good to have you home! We've missed you," my dad said, pulling me into a warm bear hug. My dad wasn't much of a conversationalist, and rarely showed any deep emotions, but I never questioned that he loved me.

Releasing me, my dad turned toward the fridge and proudly proclaimed, "I better put your mom's casserole in the oven now, before I forget. She had a few errands to run after work and won't be happy with me if dinner isn't at least in progress when she walks through the door."

"No, she won't. Which one did she make?"

"The creamy chicken one, with the asparagus and mushrooms over rice. Your favorite, of course."

"I miss her cooking. I try to make a lot of what I eat or buy better premade meals at the grocery store, but it's not the same. She would kill me if she knew I was eating out several times a week," I confessed.

"Don't worry, it's our secret. Help me out and set the table, Miss Pretty?" my dad gently requested with an adorable dad-pout.

My father had called me Miss Pretty for as long as I could remember, but usually only when it was just the two of us. It wasn't until I was fourteen and headed into the backyard to gather Tina and my dad for dinner when I overheard him calling her Miss Champion. I found out later that he called Amy Miss Brainiac.

I remember one summer when the three of us got into an ugly argument about which title was the most impressive. I didn't have any strong counterpoints as to why being pretty was better than being a champion or brainiac, though. As usual, Miss Brainiac had the best arguments.

My dad put the casserole in the oven and went to his den to drop off his briefcase. I didn't see him again until dinner. I set the table, then picked up a local magazine that was laying on the counter and read while I waited for the rest of the family to arrive home from their busy days.

Tina was the next to arrive, sweaty from the gym. She let me know that Amy was waitressing that evening and would catch up with us later. Amy was putting herself through her final year of engineering classes, and her schedule was quite overwhelming. My mom walked through the door about ten minutes after Tina.

"Ohh, how I missed you!" She grabbed me tightly and squeezed out a long, enthusiastic hug. "You look gorgeous, as usual," she said, followed by a quick peck on the cheek.

"I miss you too, Mom. It's great to be home," I said sincerely.

Instinctually after the hug, my mom spun around and opened the oven to check the progress on the casserole. She seem to know how far along it was with a simple glance, because she immediately started prepping a spring mix salad to accompany it. The rich and familiar smell of her creamy chicken delight made my stomach rumble loudly, reminding me that it had been way too long since I had eaten.

Dinner was served moments later and the majority of my family gathered at the table, as we had done for most of my childhood. Occasionally, one of my parents would need to work late and miss out, or one of my sisters would have an extracurricular activity that interfered—but for the most part, my family honored the traditional sit-down family dinner.

It felt good to be home. I devoured a larger portion than normal, and felt no shame in going back for seconds. We chatted about Tina's high school basketball team, the new flowers my mother had planted, and how my father had his worst game of golf ever to kick off the new season. Of course, they also asked plenty of questions about Nathan.

I caught myself downplaying the seriousness of the relationship while exaggerating his intellect and kindness. He had impressed my family at Christmas, and they wanted to know when he would be coming by again. Since we hadn't made official plans yet, I just said, "Don't worry; he'll be by to flatter you guys again soon." Then I redirected the conversation back to someone else's life.

It had been over seven hours since Nathan dropped me off, and I hadn't even received a text suggesting we should see each other soon. I didn't want to appear needy or insecure, but I was looking forward to having a school-free summer when we could finally enjoy more quality time together.

We lingered in the kitchen after dinner for a while, catching up as we subconsciously cleared and washed the dishes. My dad snuck away as per normal, soon followed by Tina. It was only my mother and me left in the kitchen. The happy chatter of our dinner faded, and I could see some frustration and exhaustion on my mom's face. Her eyes fluttered in an effort to keep them open.

"Everything okay, Mom?"

"I hate to cut your first day home a little short, but I'm ready to call it a night. I've been fighting a migraine all day, and I need to lie down for a bit," she reluctantly admitted. "I didn't want to abandon you on your first night home, but the drugs are not kicking in."

"Aw, that sucks you have a headache, Mom, but I understand. Go lie down, and we'll talk more later. I'm home all summer," I assured her.

Secretly, I was itching to send Nathan a text to make sure everything was still good between us. My gut was screaming that he was losing interest, which would explain the lack of affection and attention on the ride home. It's ridiculous that I could even think that when we made love that very morning, but I was wise enough to know that men are very capable of separating sex and love.

I gave my mom another long-overdue hug and retreated to my old room, while she headed on toward the master bedroom farther down the hall. It was still early enough to go out, so I decided to boldly call Nathan instead of sending him a weak, insecure text. I was hoping I would be able to seduce him into a late-night escapade.

Unfortunately, he didn't answer; I ended up rambling into his voicemail instead. "Oh, hey Nathan, it's just me. I was hoping we could hook up tonight. That's, of course, if you're free. If not, call me back and let me know the plans for tomorrow. Love you. See you soon."

I sounded fairly confident and casual, so I did my best not to overanalyze it the rest of the night, while I waited impatiently for him to call me back. I spent the next hour primping and prepping for him in case he suggested a passionate late-night tryst, but the call never came. It didn't come the following day, either.

Mindless Manipulation

I paced back and forth in the kitchen the next morning, as Amy filled me in on all the luck she was having in her search for the perfect company to work for after graduation. Female engineers were rare and she was at the top of her class, so several reputable companies were interested in adding her to their team. She was very driven, and had spent the last four years networking with engineering firms, CEOs, and city planners.

All of us are ambitious because of our mom. She stressed to us at a young age that you can make a real impact on the world, if you're willing to work for it. We admired her and followed her example, each in our own way.

"After spending time at both a private firm and a city-run agency, I'm quite certain private is the better choice. Now, I just need to wait for the offers to figure out which one is better for me. I've already ruled out McMaster and Tueche; it's definitely an old boys club," Amy concluded as she was chopping up vegetables for that evening's stew dinner. "The rest of my options have at least one woman on staff. I'd hate to be the only one."

I was supposed to be helping her sort through her choices, but I was too distracted by the lack of response from Nathan. My sister must have read my mind, because the conversation quickly changed directions.

"So, there's this cute guy in my class named Michael, whom I study with a lot. I like him, but we both agreed were too busy to actually date right now. I'm fine with it, because this semester is intense. He has potential, though. What's new with you? Still seeing Nathan?"

I nodded without making eye contact, something Amy clued into immediately.

"You don't look very enthused about it," she probed.

"No, it's good. I was just expecting that we'd get together tonight, but I haven't heard from him yet," I said, staring at my silent phone.

"Oh, give the guy a break, Katelyn," Amy responded with her usual emotionless reasoning. "He just got back home for the first time in months. I'm sure, he's anxious to see all his friends, and you can find something else to do. I'm working the late dinner shift tonight; otherwise we could do something. You should visit Rachel instead and play it cool with him."

"Yeah, of course. No big deal." I shrugged it off and took Amy's advice. Rachel was spending time with her parents and had a date night scheduled with Chris, so we made plans for coffee and yoga the following afternoon.

Since everyone else was busy, I went for a run around the trails by my parents' house. I had barely been running over the last few months and it showed, in both my endurance and speed. I desperately tried not to think about him, but was convinced there would be a message on my phone as soon as I returned from the run. Nope, nothing.

I took a long, hot shower after I got home and took more time than usual to blow dry and style my thick hair. I intentionally left my phone in my bedroom while I was in the bathroom. Once again, I assumed he would have called by the time I got dressed.

I helped make and enjoyed a lovely stew dinner with my parents, followed by chatting in the kitchen with my mom and Tina. Even though it had been months since we'd cooked together, we flowed smoothly as always. I made a promise to myself that I would cook more with Nathan once we got back to Toronto.

Around nine o'clock, Tina left to see a few friends and my mom snuck off to read her latest mystery novel before bed. I spent the remainder of my evening filling my dad in on my classes, major projects, and teachers as he pretended to listen with one eye glued to the hockey game on the TV.

There was still no answer from Nathan when I finally gave up and went to bed for the night.

I had a little wine with my mom when we made dinner, another glass after dinner, and a third while I chatted with my dad. I wasn't drunk, but my imagination kicked into overdrive as soon as I closed my eyes.

For some reason, I started thinking that no one in Nathan's house would know to contact me, if something bad happened to him. It didn't make sense that he would go a full day without returning my message. I hadn't seen or heard from him since he dropped me off over thirty hours before.

I tossed and turned until well after midnight, crashing from exhaustion at some point. I was relieved I chose sleep over a late-night call to Nathan demanding to know why he hadn't returned my call. When I awoke, I decided that I would text him early in the afternoon. One more time to check in, and I'd only worry if I didn't get a response by then.

Hey. Everything okay? Did you get my message?

I stared at the message for a few minutes before hitting *send*. It had been well over twenty-four hours since I left the previous message, and it was a fair question. We were a couple in an intimate relationship, so why did I feel frightened by his possible reaction?

I couldn't take my eyes off the phone for the seven minutes that it took Nathan to text me back. Fortunately, my fears were unfounded, and there was no horrible or traumatic reason for his delayed response.

Yes, sorry. I was just about to message you when I saw this. You free this afternoon?

In fact, there was no explanation ever given, but mainly because I never pushed the question. I did wait several minutes before responding, as I didn't want to seem desperate by jumping at his initial invitation. Plus, I wouldn't cancel on my best friend for him.

I have plans already. How about tonight? Dinner?

Almost immediately, Nathan replied: *I'm going to a party, but you can come.*

His wording made me feel like my invitation was an afterthought. I paced my room for five minutes, trying to come up with an appropriate reply. He was being distant, and I didn't want to seem overly pushy. We hadn't really defined our relationship to any degree, although in my opinion the sex and "I love you" meant it was a serious commitment.

Finally, I texted: *Sure, what time?*

Pick you up around 9.

I typed *great*, first with an exclamation point and then without. The exclamation seemed too excited, the period made it sound sarcastic or insincere. I was going to text *sounds great* or *looking forward to it*, but his brief replies made me feel like I needed to be just as aloof. After some internal debate, I settled on *OK*.

It didn't go as great as I hoped, but at least I enjoyed myself during the rest of the afternoon. (It's always awesome catching up with Rachel.) I didn't realize how much I missed her, until I saw her burst through the yoga studio doors with a giant smile on her beautiful face. We gave each other a long squeeze before setting up our mats.

Our quiet and healthy class was followed by a boisterous coffee and sinful pastries at our favorite cafe. We talked so much that three hours passed in what seemed like a matter of minutes. Even when we realized it was time to head to our respective homes for dinner, we gabbed non-stop in what turned out to be a thirty-minute goodbye.

I gave her all the positive updates on Nathan, including the impressive sexual adventures. However, I left out the recent hiccups. I felt certain we would be back to our normal, loving relationship after spending time together that evening. A little distance makes the heart grow fonder, right?

It was after 6:30 when I got home, and my family dinner was practically done. My father was drinking his coffee in the living room, watching a Montreal semi-final playoff game. As a Canadian border city with Detroit, this meant most people were either Red Wing or Toronto Maple Leaf fans. Neither team stood a chance of winning, and my dad rarely rooted for an underdog.

My mom and sisters were chatting while subconsciously picking at a tray of brownies Amy had made everyone for dessert. "Help yourself to some dinner and brownies. I assume you and Rachel lost track of time catching up."

"Of course we did. I missed her. I'm not overly hungry, but I can't resist that chocolate goodness."

I joined their circle, but was too lost in my own thoughts to truly participate in their debate over whether Tina should become a police officer or work for the border patrol. I didn't know that she had settled on a career path, or that she wanted such a dangerous job. As a kid, she was going to be a veterinarian, and then it was a sports broadcaster. Tina was a hard worker and in great physical condition, so I figured she'd excel at whatever job she chose.

I still had plenty of time to get ready, but I couldn't fake being calm any longer. My legs were recklessly bouncing under the table as I nibbled on the edge of a fingernail. I finally excused myself from the kitchen after Tina called me out for staring blankly at the fridge. I was mentally scanning my memory for the sexiest outfit I owned and hadn't heard any of the recent conversation.

Once again, I was worried Nathan was losing interest. I put on a silky black thong, my sexist black push-up bra, and a tight, low cut t-shirt with strategically-torn jeans. I teased out my hair to give it more volume and decided to forgo comfort for a pair of strappy high heels that I normally only endured on special occasions. Something felt off, and I wanted to recapture the passion we so recently shared.

Nathan was twenty minutes late, driving his mom's car. He came to the door, gave me a quick kiss on the cheek as soon as we stepped outside, and held the front door for me. I noticed there was a couple I hadn't met before already waiting in the backseat, and since he neglected to introduce me, I took it upon myself to do so once we pulled out of the driveway.

"Hey, I'm Katelyn," I said as I peeked into the back to see who exactly was there. I noticed the woman had short, dark hair and wore a black leather jacket, and was staring out the driver's side window. A noticeably shorter guy with light brown hair stared directly back at me.

"I'm Alan, this is Trish." He made a quick hand gesture towards the woman I assumed was his date. She gave me a quick nod of acknowledgement. Neither appeared interested in conversing with me any further.

Nathan quickly added, "We still have to pick up one more friend. The party is outside of town, in the county, so it's easier if we take one car."

"Sure, that's great!" I responded with an eager smile.

"I should have asked early, but if everyone drinks and there's no one to drive back, are you cool crashing there? We can sleep it off in the car," Nathan said, as if it was regular occurrence.

The thought hadn't dawned on me, but I wasn't planning on drinking enough to get drunk, so I offered to be the designated driver instead. Nathan was more than eager to accept and then suggested that I could crash at his house afterwards. He would drive me home in the morning. I wasn't sure how my parents would feel about me staying there. However, I was an adult, and knew it would be my choice.

While I was pondering my response to his invitation, Nathan pulled into the driveway of our fifth passenger. Just like he had done with me, he got out of the car and walked up the driveway to the front door. I was surprised to see that it was another woman we were picking up, but figured she must be a friend of Trish's.

She pulled her wind-swept blonde hair away from her face before greeting Nathan with a quick kiss on his cheek. From a distance, it looked relatively innocent. I squashed any initial feelings of jealousy or insecurity, and chose to brush it off as nothing. Our newest party-goer hopped in the backseat behind me and immediately introduced herself with an excited energy the other occupants lacked.

"Hello! I'm Jeannie. Thanks for letting me ride with you guys." Her voice was friendly and encouraging.

"I'm Alan, this is Trish."

The words "I'm Katelyn," slipped out of my mouth in a meek almost-whisper. I was thrown off by Alan giving Jeannie the same monotone introduction I had received. I'd assumed she was joining us because of them. However, just like me, she was a guest of Nathan's.

"It's all right seeing the family after being away at school, but I was ready to bolt. I've had a taste of freedom now and no desire to be stuck at home with them," Jeannie continued, addressing no one in particular.

Nathan was quick to chime in. "The first night was manageable, but now I come up with an excuse to leave the house every thirty minutes or so. It's going to be a long summer if my mom doesn't start spending more time at her boyfriend's." I saw him look over his shoulder in her direction.

"At least there should be some wild parties." Jeannie lifted her eyebrows suggestively at Nathan, then smiled at me.

I politely smiled back, as nonchalantly as possible. My brain was trying to label their relationship, and I took my position in the front seat as reassurance that she couldn't be more than just a good friend. I am not so insecure that I would deny the man I love an important friendship simply because the person happens to be an attractive woman. Right?

A popular song that I can no longer recall the name of came on and Nathan turned up the volume. Jeannie sang quietly in the backseat. I stared straight ahead as my mind ran in circles. As the song was ending, we pulled up alongside a row of cars straddling both sides of a county ditch. A large old farmhouse and even bigger barn waited at the end of the long, loose-stone driveway.

After we parked, we made the hike through both soft grass and wobbly stones (neither of which suited the heels I was attempting to walk in) to the crowded barn. I noticed Trish had on a cute pair of ballet slipper-style flats and Jeannie was wearing Converse low tops with slim-fitting jeans. I was the only one struggling.

Nathan did walk beside me, at least. He led me toward the keg at the back of the barn and offered to pour me a glass. As he was filling my cup, Jeannie rounded the corner and caught his attention by shouting, "Pour me one too, Nate." While he was distracted, my cup overflowed. He shook off the excess foam and handed me the wet, sticky plastic cup. He grabbed another and filled it for Jeannie, then filled one for himself.

"So, Nate tells me you met at University. What program are you in?" Jeannie's use of Nate caught me off guard. I had heard a few of his friends call him that, but I preferred Nathan. I thought it made him sound more mature and sophisticated. In hindsight, I had never asked him what he preferred. I'd assumed he wouldn't want his name abbreviated, based on my own annoyance over being called Kate.

The only time anyone called me Kate was when I was being scolded or lectured. My dad would say, "Think it through, Kate," when he felt I was making a bad decision. My mom would call me Katie, which I loathed, whenever she was encouraging me to be less fussy about men, "Katie, there's no such thing as a perfect man. Just look for someone who seems perfect to you."

I made a point of introducing myself to everyone I met as Katelyn, and I always used my full name on paperwork, greeting cards, and school assignments. When people had the courtesy to ask my preference, of course I would say Katelyn. I should have thought to ask Nathan if he would rather be called Nate.

I must have been lost in my head for longer than socially acceptable, because she was now staring at me, confused. I blurted out, "Fashion design," just as Nathan muttered, "She's in fashion."

"Wow, that's pretty cool. Did you design this?" she asked, pointing out my plain shirt and basic jeans.

"Oh no, I was just looking for something casual tonight. I design more retro chic party dresses."

"I'd love to see your stuff sometime." She sounded a bit too chipper to be sincere.

"Sure! Are you in school, Jeannie?" I returned her fake enthusiasm.

"I took the year off to work on a cruise ship, which sounded a lot more fun than it ended up being. It was still a great experience, and I got a lot of sun. Now I'm working part time at my aunt's travel agency while deciding if this is the industry for me. I want to spend my life on vacation. I'll probably waste every dollar I make on wild trips around the world," she rambled on, her face beaming with confidence.

I appreciated her candor, and we chatted a bit about some of the places she'd seen and excursions she'd gone on. My parents took us to Disneyland when I was a kid, and we went to Cedar Pointe a few times in high school, but nothing compared to her stories. Nathan, or Nate, was just as enthralled by her wild escapades as I, which took me several minutes to notice due to the spell she had me under. She would be an exceptional salesperson for a travel company.

Around the same time that I noticed that he was looking directly in her eyes, I realized she was just as focused on him. The conversation started with me and turned toward Nathan. I was careful not to overreact and played it as cool as I could.

"Wow, I can't see any bad side to working on a cruise ship. It sounds amazing," I interjected at the next pause between her drunk Hawaii luau story, where she fell asleep on the beach, and whatever bold adventure she planned on sharing next.

"I missed home and solid ground. I'd rather tour Europe or Asia. Plus, it sucked catering to the insane guests and their whiney demands. I'm glad I did it, but I'm not sure if I'd go away for so long on a cruise again."

"Yeah, but now *I* want to do it," Nathan said, almost flirtatiously. I was trying so hard not to let jealousy feed my judgment.

"Well, it might be worth doing again if I went with a good friend. I felt empowered doing it on my own, but it gets lonely after the first few weeks. I was craving a familiar face."

Nathan gave her a pouty face and I suddenly felt like I was the third wheel. I sipped my beer in silence while they began to reminiscence and tell countless stories of the crazy things they did in high school. I wished Nathan would have talked about her before the party, so I would know if they had once dated. It would be cruel of him to flirt with an ex-girlfriend, if that was what was happening.

They were not exactly complimenting each other, or making plans to hook up. There was no touching or anything truly alarming. My gut sensed they had a connection, though, and I was fighting back the urge to react to it for what felt like hours. It was probably closer to twenty minutes before Jeannie finally welcomed me back into the conversation.

"Kate, you must be a beer drinker!" She glanced down at my empty glass. Both of their sixteen-ounce cups were still half-full.

"Not really; I prefer wine. This just went down a bit too fast." My cheeks were flushed from both the warmth of chugging a beer and the embarrassment of her noticing.

"I have a bottle of vodka in my purse, since I knew there would only be beer. I'll make us vodka waters." Jeannie grabbed two new cups and told us to follow her. She led us through a door at the end of the barn, down a path lined with shiny stones, and into a side entrance to the house on the east side of the barn.

I wasn't much of a drinker, especially vodka, but felt pressured to go with the flow. "Sounds great," slipped from my lips without knowing if I was sure. I watched her pour, and the vodka in my cup filled over one-third of the cup, while hers was only filled less than a fifth with alcohol.

Although the beer went down fast, I was careful to sip the vodka. I didn't want to lose my senses, at least not until I could figure out exactly why I was spending the evening watching my boyfriend talk to some smoking hot world traveler all night. My imagination kept resorting to jealousy, so I scooped up Nathan's hand in mine, demonstrating to the real third wheel that he was mine.

I could tell he felt awkward about it, and immediately regretted my decision. I casually let it slip back out, while practically shouting, "So, introduce me to the rest of your friends. Whose house is this?"

"It's this guy Mark's, from high school. Let's walk around and see who I know." Nathan headed back outside, leading me along the pathway and back into the barn. He introduced me to more people than I could remember names for, although I did mentally note that he never once referred to me as his girlfriend. I worried that we had two very different interpretations of our relationship—something that obviously occurs quite often in college.

Jeannie would get sidetracked in conversations with other people, but would eventually gravitate back to Nathan. I felt very aware of her all night. I could tell she was monitoring me just as closely when she pointed out that I had barely touched my vodka water.

"If you don't like the drink I made, please don't feel obligated to drink it," she offered kindly.

"I told Nathan that I would drive us home, and that tasted like a lot of vodka. I just met most of you, and I don't want to put us in a ditch," I added with a laugh, so I didn't sound snarky.

"Smart! Nate needs a responsible influence in his life. Someone to keep him out of trouble." Her words were accompanied by a look that implied there was so much more to that story. My puzzled expression, urging her to expand on that thought, prompted her to quickly whisper in my ear, "Just stay smart enough not to put up with his shit."

The tone of her voice was deep and foreboding. The words on their own felt harmless, but her breath on my neck gave me goosebumps. Later, I rationalized that it had to be her way of trying to break us up, so she could make her move.

Just as she pulled away from me, Nathan redirected his attention to our conversation and Jeannie's expression instantly went back to the bubbly woman I met earlier. I wondered if he heard her or noticed her leaning toward my ear.

"Do you want me to add more water? Come with me; we'll fix it." She quickly changed the subject, sporting an exaggerated smile. This time it was Jeannie scooping up my hand, and Nathan quickly intercepting it.

"I'll take her in the kitchen to fix the drink. Spend some time with your other friends." Nathan sounded surprisingly stern.

Jeannie turned around and walked away without so much as a look in our direction. That, combined with the coldness in his tone, assured me that she wasn't a threat to our relationship. In fact, we didn't see Jeannie again until Nathan gathered us for the ride home. She told us to leave without her, because she'd found another ride home. I had almost let my insecurities ruin my entire night for nothing.

I briefly debated if Jeannie was legitimately trying to warn me about something; if that was the case, it most likely had to do with his pot smoking. I've seen him smoke marijuana a few times with some of his friends at university. He had paused to take a hit from a guy when we were going between the house and the barn. I wasn't bothered by it.

I knew a lot of pot smokers in high school, and we'd spent enough time together that I would know if he was a burnout. I convinced myself that Jeannie either wanted "Nate" for herself and was feeling rejected, or she was trying to warn me that he liked marijuana. Neither concerned me enough to give it a second thought. We dropped off Alan and Trish before heading to his place. As soon as they were out of the car, he made his feelings for me obvious.

"I loved showing you off tonight. Every guy there must have been jealous. I'm craving that smoking hot body of yours. Are you staying at my house?"

"Your mom won't mind?" I asked.

"My mom won't notice," he answered.

"Mine will notice if I'm not home, which means I need to call and it's so late to call there."

"You're an adult."

"Yes, but they are expecting me. They wouldn't care if I'd told them earlier that I wouldn't be home," I said, trying to justify my hesitation.

"You're such a goody-goody," Nathan teased.

"Sorry, but I know my family and I don't want them to worry."

"Why didn't you tell them earlier? Didn't we discuss it on the ride to the party? Just send a text saying you don't have a ride home. They'll understand," he begged.

The pressure he was putting on me was tainting his prior compliments. However, we'd only had one passionate exchange in the past week, and I didn't want to turn him down. I eventually caved and texted my sister to put a note on the kitchen island, and quietly followed Nathan inside his house.

The house was silent and dark. We felt our way through the foyer and front room before he turned on a hallway light. This time he reached out for my hand, leading me into his room and then onto his twin bed.

I melted as his full lips pressed themselves against mine. I could feel his rock-solid penis pressing against my anxious clit. We ripped our clothes off one another, just like you see in the movies. I slowly dragged my mouth along his cock before we started fucking so hard his bed was bouncing loudly off the wall.

A few brief minutes later (before I climaxed), he came loudly and flopped onto the bed next to me. We made so much noise that I was worried his mother would be busting the door down any second, and I couldn't concentrate. It felt extra forbidden and exciting, doing it in his parents' home.

It wasn't until the next morning that we found out she'd spent the night at her new boyfriend's apartment. Just like the note I asked Tina to write on my behalf, there was a note pinned to their fridge with a magnet. All it said was: *Chad's picked me up for dinner. Back tomorrow.*

Her lack of detail didn't phase him. I was used to detailed notes from my mother, about what I could heat up for dinner and exactly when she would be back. She'd wish me a good night and sign it *Love, Mom.* I doubt that kind of stuff really matters to boys.

Nathan offered me instant coffee and a ride home. No snuggling in bed or other romantic gestures, but I was quickly learning that it was foolish to expect anything more. Every romantic comedy I watched growing up was a load of shit. The guys I know don't have the sensitivity or creativity to write a full sentence text about how they feel, let alone a poem or a love song.

I went home disappointed, and most of the summer continued along a similar cycle. Nathan would go anywhere from four to six days with no contact or responses, then suddenly we'd plan a date night or he'd take me to a party. We would wind up making passionate love at his house, then revert back to an awkward silence for several days. I wanted more from the relationship, and I'd thought we had already reached the point of true love. The way things were going, I feared he would run from me if I pushed the issue.

Up in Smoke

S ummer flew by and with a week left until school started, everything drastically changed. I hadn't heard from Nathan in eight days, and was trying to arrange my ride back to University. I had sent him three brief text messages over the past week, then left a message on the Monday night, one week before we were back in class. Finally, at 10:00 a.m. on Tuesday, I got a text.

Can we go for a drive? We need to talk.

My gut ached, sensing this was the infamous breakup meeting. He wanted to end it before we went back to University. I waited almost fifteen minutes before responding. Not knowing for certain if I was about to be dumped or how I should respond, I simply replied, *K*.

Be there in ten minutes, Nathan texted back.

I hadn't showered yet, nor had I bothered to put on a bra. I kicked it into overdrive and spruced myself up as fast I could. If his intention was to dump me, how I looked wouldn't matter. The last moments we had shared together involved him shaking uncontrollably with joy, so I couldn't understand why he would want to break up and was trying hard not to jump to that conclusion.

He pulled into my parents' driveway in his mom's car, and waited for me to come outside. I could tell he was upset. He mumbled something about finding a spot to talk and then pulled back onto the street rather quickly.

Neither of us said a word the entire fifteen minutes that it took to get to the parking lot along the waterfront. The radio volume was intentionally cranked up too loud for us to talk. He pulled into a space far away from the other cars, rolled down the window, and turned the car off. I could see pain in his eyes when he finally turned in my direction.

"This weekend, I went camping with some friends. It was most of my graduating class, guys and girls. Everyone drank a lot. I drank a lot and got high, too. Things got out of control." The words spilled from his lips as if he was confessing to a crime.

He took a long pause to stare at the floor of the car. My sinking gut thought it knew where the conversation was headed. Some girl threw herself at him, and he "accidentally" cheated on me. I patiently waited for his excuses and apology. If he'd slept with someone else, I had to end our relationship. I wouldn't respect myself if I stayed with someone who couldn't be faithful. That was the bottom line for me.

His fingers were trembling and the silence dragged on. He looked genuinely distraught, but I refused to let his guilt soften my reaction. Alcohol is not an excuse, and neither is temptation. If he loved me, he wouldn't cheat under any circumstances.

"Jeannie is dead," Nathan blurted out, shattering my train of thought into a million pieces.

My mind was still trying to process his possible infidelity. I was blindsided by the real news. "What? How? *Dead?*" Each word trickled sloppily from my lips.

"She was drunk, must have passed out by the campfire. It was still lit. Somehow, she went up in flames while everyone was sleeping." His lip trembled and his eyes glossed over with tears.

I gasped in genuine horror: the stench, the excruciating pain, and fiery debris. People say being burned alive is one of the worst ways to die, although it's surprisingly not as awful as a person would imagine. I know better now, but at that point in time I didn't know how someone would react to the flames. I envisioned Jeannie screaming at the top of her lungs, writhing in pain as the flames swallowed her whole. *How did no one hear her?* I wondered.

"They couldn't save her? You guys called an ambulance, right?"

"Olivia did in the morning, after we found her burnt body. It didn't even look like her. We knew it was her because of her fucking fluorescent pink runners. You could see the pink, just charred black and neon pink." Nathan's fingers danced rapidly on the car steering wheel, even though the music was no longer playing.

"I'm so sorry, Nathan." I wrapped my arms around him. He didn't break down and cry, but it was obvious he was in a state of shock.

"Thank you, Kate. Hey, you can call me Nate. Nate and Kate. I like that," he said with a childlike smile. For the first time in my life, I actually liked the idea of being Kate.

He invited me back to his place, where we almost instantly celebrated that we were still alive. I've heard how the death of someone can inspire feverish passion. This was certainly one of those cases. Nate drilled me from behind, tightly gripping my shoulder and slamming himself inside me.

After Nate's final victorious thrust and moan of fulfillment, we flopped on top of the bed and held each other until we fell asleep. It wasn't even noon, yet a long nap felt necessary. The news of what happened to Jeannie was heartbreaking; resting in his arms was soothing.

The next day, Nate insisted on going back to Toronto as soon as possible. He needed to clear his head before the semester started, and couldn't stomach attending her funeral. He was my boyfriend, so in spite of their disappointment, my parents understood why I would leave early as well. Dave and Kassie wanted to spend the extra days with their families, so they decided to drive up separately on Sunday.

Nate picked me up early Thursday morning in his mom's car. When I'd asked him the night before why she was letting him drive it to Toronto, he mumbled something about buying it off of her for dirt cheap. It was a rusted old 2004 Neon, and he told me she had decided it was time for a new car.

Nate looked like he hadn't slept, and the two empty bottles of Five Star Energy drink on the floor of the car confirmed my suspicions. I offered to drive, but he wouldn't hear of it. He tried to make small talk and gave me a compliment on how I looked, but I could tell his mind was elsewhere. I was trying to convince myself that it was immature to be jealous simply because he was brokenhearted over the death of another woman. They were obviously friends, and she was no longer a threat to our relationship.

We drove non-stop again. Fortunately, I was able to make it the entire four-and-a-half-hour drive without needing to pee. I barely made it to the washroom in time, once we got to his place. I was hungry the entire car ride as well, but didn't want to ask him to stop. This time I had at least eaten a full breakfast of eggs, bacon, and toast before leaving my parents' house.

I could tell he was distraught, or at least terribly shaken up, over Jeannie's death. I was worried that saying the wrong thing could further upset him; saying nothing was safer. I waited until we were settled back in at his place before I attempted to broach the subject.

"I'm so sorry about Jeannie, truly. What a horrible accident. If you want to talk about it, I'll listen." I kissed his cheek and held his hand

"I just want to forget about it. Please." He squeezed my hand quickly, then let it go and went to the fridge to grab a beer. He finished it in a matter of moments, not saying a word in between sips. He grabbed a second and flopped himself on the couch. "I'm tired from driving. Do you want to watch TV?"

"Yes, sure." I grabbed a bottle of water and joined him. It was still early in the afternoon and I wasn't ready to drink away my problems, especially considering I hadn't eaten since breakfast. I wasn't going to judge him if he wanted to get hammered. I had never lost anyone that close to me, and wasn't sure how I'd react.

We wasted the rest of the day eating the chips and cookies we'd scored from his mom's house and drinking every ounce of alcohol that the boys kept at their place. Nate also smoked some weed; he snuck outside when he got up to go to the bathroom. However, he was unsuccessful at hiding the smell. We never discussed it and it wasn't a problem in our relationship—at that time.

I turned my mobile phone off after texting my mom that we had arrived safely. When I turned it on the next morning, I saw I missed four phone calls and nearly a dozen texts from my mom, Amy, Rachel, and

Tina. Not one specified the reason behind their persistence, just asked me to call ASAP. My mind was racing as I called my mom from Nate and Dave's kitchen, wondering who else must have died.

"Katelyn, are you alone right now?" were the first words out of my mom's mouth.

"Um, yes. Nate's in the other room."

"You need to leave. The police are coming to interview him. He's a suspect in a murder." My mom's voice cracked between words.

"What? That's impossible. Who are they saying he killed?"

"A girl at a party. It looked like she was burned, but they said she was beaten really badly before the fire. People heard her fighting with Nathan. They were all asked to stay in the city in case they needed to be interviewed, yet he takes off the very next day, before her funeral. It looks highly suspicious. The police have been trying to reach him and he's not answering his phone," my mom frantically spewed.

"We fell asleep with our phones off. He's devastated about her death. He didn't do it. All he knows is she fell in a fire. Mom, trust me, Nate's innocent."

"He needs to talk to the police," my mother urged.

"He will, Mom. Relax. He's not a violent guy. Trust me, I know." I meant what I said—at least back then I did.

"Did you know he stole his mother's car to get to Toronto?"

"He bought it off her," I argued.

"She reported it stolen," Mom insisted otherwise.

"He's not a bad guy. I'm sure it's a misunderstanding," I persisted, still defending him.

"I hope so. I love you. Please be safe," my mom pleaded.

"I will. Don't worry. Love you too."

I hung up before she could say anything more. I relayed her message to Nate, and he sincerely looked shocked. Without a moment's hesitation, he turned on his phone and called the Windsor police officer's number.

The police wanted him to return to Windsor for an interview, but he argued that he was innocent and devastated over the loss of his friend. He explained that he left because he needed to clear his head, so he was ready to focus on school. Nate said he couldn't afford the expense or time to travel back to Windsor, and begged the detective to allow the Toronto Police to interview him instead.

I listened to his side of the conversation, and he sounded like a reasonable, sane person. The trained detective must have thought so as well, because he agreed to make an exception. As soon as Nate hung up, we drove down to the closest police station together. I waited outside while he was interviewed by two officers for over twenty minutes.

Neither of the officers who interviewed him felt like he was guilty of anything, so we were home within an hour. He told me that they didn't even ask about his mom's car, because it obviously wasn't stolen, and they were only investigating him because he took off so quickly.

I sent my mom a text, simply saying: *He talked to the police, he's innocent and everything is fine.*

She sent me one back asking me to call her, but I didn't. I didn't want to discuss it any further. I was shocked that my boyfriend would even be considered a murderer and a little annoyed that my mother would jump to that conclusion. I was riled up and needed to vent, and knew Rachel would understand.

"I'm going to head home for awhile, get caught up on laundry and catch up with Rachel," I called out over to Nate, who was in the kitchen making a stack of turkey and mayo sandwiches. He told me once that adding lettuce and tomato was a waste of time, despite me saying that I thought it was a necessity on any good sandwich.

"Don't take off so fast. I made us sandwiches. I would really appreciate your company. The interrogation was awful. I could never hurt anyone, especially a woman. Please stay." His sad and noticeably tired eyes were calling out to me.

"Sure, I can stay. Sorry, I didn't realize you were so upset."

"How could you not know? Think! *Fuck*," Nate snapped, as he shoved the plate of bread and meat in my face. "My friend died. People think I did it. Wouldn't you be upset? I thought my girlfriend would have my back. You do believe me, right?"

"Of course I believe you!" I exclaimed.

"Good; I couldn't bear it if you didn't. I love you, Kate." He wrapped his arms around my waist and begun kissing me passionately. His lips suckling on my neck, just below my ears, made me quiver. I felt horrible for not supporting him, and showed my remorse the best way I knew how. I turned down the boring sandwiches, dropped to my knees, and helped myself to a mouthful of his, now fully erect penis. Nate's mood suddenly improved.

I stayed at his place until Dave came back two days later. We didn't discuss Jeannie or the police again. Nate started drinking early in the morning both days, and was passed out shortly after we ate dinner. Even though he had some groceries, we both felt too lazy to cook and ordered out. I was eating crap and feeling it, so I decided my first priority when I got back to my place would be to eat a salad and exercise.

Unfortunately, Kassie and Rachel interrupted my plans. Kassie was first, and started hammering me within minutes of walking in the door. Jeannie's death had made the London news, and Dave had filled her in on Nate being a suspect. She said that Dave was nervous about going back to the apartment with Nate.

"Give me a break, Kassie! Nate's not a violent guy! He wouldn't hurt anyone!" I shouted in his defense.

"How do you know that? Dave has seen him lose his temper over nothing. Several people at he party heard him arguing with her. Dave heard they hooked up this summer."

"Bullshit! I know he's not violent because I spend a lot of time with him, and he never really loses his cool. We've all yelled at someone out of frustration before and had arguments with people. He went to the police station; they believed he was innocent, and so do I!" I hollered back at Kassie before storming off to my bedroom.

Within minutes of entering my room, my phone rang. It was Rachel, which reminded me that I hadn't returned her earlier messages and I didn't want to piss her off by not answering now. She knew her worth and had plenty of friends. Rachel wouldn't chase me if I started ignoring her; I didn't want to risk losing her friendship, so I answered.

I regretted my choice almost immediately. Rachel had the same concerns as my mom and Kassie. The first thing she said after I apologized was, "I'm just relieved to hear your voice. Have you left him for good?"

"No. He didn't do it, Rachel. The cops agreed he's innocent and I'm tired of defending him to everyone." My defenses kicked in.

"He smashed her face in so hard her nose cartilage was compressed into her skull."

"The guy who killed Jeannie did that. Nate didn't kill her," I corrected her assumption.

"Are you sure? There weren't any other suspects," she persisted.

"Yes. He's not violent. He's broken up over her death. They were friends." My tone was as controlled as I could manage, while my heart raced rapidly.

"Just be careful. I don't want to lose you," Rachel responded sincerely.

"You won't," I promised, fully intending to always keep it.

It was reassuring to hear she valued our friendship as much as I did. We switched the topic to Chris and then school before wishing each other a great semester, and promising to see each other at Thanksgiving. Just as we were saying our goodbyes, she added one last warning.

"Promise me you'll leave him at the first sign of violence?"

"Yeah, obviously. Please stop worrying."

"Fine. I know you're smart enough not to fall for an asshole. Talk soon."

"Yep! Stop worrying. Ciao bella."

I didn't want to go back in the living room and continue my unpleasant discussion with Kassie and there wasn't enough room around my bed for a decent workout, so I took a nap instead. I was exhausted from the drama and binge drinking. I needed to rejuvenate my mind and body before classes started up again.

The school semester was off to a good start and everyone had settled back into their routine. Nate agreed that we both needed to focus on our schoolwork, so we only saw each other from Friday night to Sunday afternoon. I would stay at his place, while Dave stayed at ours. It was easy to keep my promise to Rachel, since Nate was being exceptionally sweet. Even when he was drunk or stoned, he would be really playful and silly.

I loved him. There was no doubt in my mind, I could spend the rest of my life as Nate and Kate. Prior to Thanksgiving, I asked my mom which day she would be making her big turkey dinner so that I could invite Nate to join us. I knew if they spent more time with him, they would feel foolish for thinking he could ever harm someone.

Unfortunately, yet fortunately for Nate, our Thanksgiving dinner plans didn't work out. The day before the four of us were supposed to hit the road and travel south to see our families, Nate was scouted by a real modeling agency.

He had gone shopping with another guy from his program in downtown Toronto. They were trying on jeans when an attractive older man tapped him on the shoulder. The guy gave Nate his business card, and said he could use him in the background of an ad that was being shot that weekend. The gig paid $300, so there was no way I could ask Nate to miss out on the opportunity.

I went back to Windsor without him. My parents were skeptical at the reason behind his absence and still pushed the rumor that Nate played a role in Jeannie's shocking death. I insisted he was innocent, and assured them it was a legit modeling job. He had never given me any reason to doubt him.

Nate promised to take me to an upscale restaurant for dinner the Saturday after Thanksgiving with the money he earned. I didn't think that anyone would question his ability to be mistaken for a model. Just as I was always pretty, Nate always looked like he belonged on a magazine cover.

I spent Friday evening with my family, Saturday with Rachel, and then enjoyed a traditional Thanksgiving dinner with my family on Sunday before heading back to Toronto on Monday morning.

I had sent Nate two texts over the weekend, but he had not replied to either. I assumed he was in a whirlwind of excitement with his new career possibility. He always said his ultimate goal was fame and fortune through the entertainment industry, in any role that fit. I would never stand in the way of his dreams.

Nate was bursting with energy when I got back, and had already mapped out a plan to take his supermodel potential to the next level. The agent he'd met offered him more commercial work in New York, which was only a short flight away. By the time I got back to Toronto, he was packing to leave again the following day.

When he sent me a text saying that he would soon be gone again, I invited myself to his place Monday night to discuss it further. I was hoping we could celebrate together, enjoying the fancy dinner he promised, but there wasn't enough time.

"Where will you be staying in New York?"

"Ryan has a condo where he lets out-of-town models stay while they're working in New York. I can stay there for free, as long as there's work for me." He explained with a goofy grin on his face.

"You're going to be living with strangers? Do you trust this guy?" I was struggling to share in his excitement.

"He's a professional, and he thinks I have the look of a cover model. I want this so badly; I'll do whatever it takes to make it happen!" Nate insisted.

"I understand why you want to go, but was hoping we could discuss our future before you took off. I missed you after a weekend away. I don't want to lose you to New York," I confessed to him, which was followed by a long, warm embrace.

"I'll miss you too, but I can make a thousand bucks in a weekend in New York. It's way more than I would make working an entire week here at the bar. I can't pass this up," he explained.

"Are you just working the one week? When are you coming back?"

"Don't know, because I plan on accepting any job that's offered. This is what I've been waiting for since I moved here. This is what I've always wanted to happen."

"I want this for you too. What about school? You can't drop out." The fear of him leaving for good made me sound desperate.

"Truth is, I wasn't doing very well in my classes. I hated the program. Be happy for me, Kate. Once I'm established, you can quit school and move in with me."

"I don't want to quit school. I want to be a designer, and school is a critical part of my success."

"There's no better city to be a fashion designer in than New York! Isn't it the fashion capital of the world? You could learn a lot more as an apprentice, working for a real designer," Nate countered.

I couldn't argue with that point in particular. I didn't want to continue fighting, considering he would be leaving soon. Instead I gave him a long, sensual kiss, which as per usual, led to so much more. I was extra loud and appreciative to leave him with a lasting memory for however long he chose to stay in New York. There was a connection we shared that I wasn't willing to let go of easily.

At first, Nate didn't appear to be as devastated by our time apart as I felt. I couldn't stop thinking about him from the moment he left, but he was too enamored with his new, flashy lifestyle. I called him every day for updates, and listened to him go on and on about how much fun he was having and all the modeling possibilities.

He was supposed to come to visit the first weekend, but cancelled at the last minute because he ended up having to work. I was going to visit him the second weekend, but he cancelled again; he was sleeping on a couch at a new friend's house, and there wasn't enough room for me. He said Ryan's condo was too crowded, so he'd moved out.

"Are you still working for Ryan?" I enquired, genuinely concerned about his turbulent living arrangements.

"I'm working for a bunch of different people. I'm the new talent, so there's lots of interest. Ryan wanted me to be exclusive to him, but I just couldn't commit. I can't tie myself down this early in the game," Nate explained.

"So, you're making good money? You sound happy."

"I couldn't be happier! Well, unless you were here with me. I miss you. If you had a job here, we'd have enough to afford renting someplace of our own. If I found you a job in fashion, would you move here with me?" Nate asked.

"I would love to live with you, once I graduate," I replied.

"Fuck school, Kate! We're better than that. We can gain everything we need to know through real life experience," he argued passionately.

"My parents would disown me if I dropped out of school without a solid opportunity in New York."

"Stop living for your parents. It's time for you to start living the life you want."

"Well, then it would need to be the right opportunity for me," I corrected my requirements.

"Well then, I'm going to find you a job that's too good to turn down," he proclaimed.

That was the first of several similar conversations, and he became more persistent the longer we were apart. Finally, on the fourth weekend, we decided to split the cost on a fancy hotel room for two nights, so we could be together. I had picked up quite a few extra shifts waitressing, since Nate took off to New York. Working at the café helped the time pass, and now it gave me the means to afford a much-needed getaway.

Romance Reignited

Nate made the arrangements for the hotel and I took care of my transportation. I booked a flight out of Toronto 7:25 Friday morning with a return flight at 2:35 p.m. on Sunday. I only had two classes on Friday, and hadn't missed either so far that semester. I wanted to see him so badly that I didn't feel the slightest bit guilty for skipping school. He occupied every inch of my mind from the moment the flight was booked.

The plane landed at 9:18 a.m., which was a few minutes before I told Nate to be there. I'd paid extra for the non-stop flight so we'd have more time together. I gathered my luggage and waited by the front entrance, as we'd agreed upon. I had asked him to be there at 9:30 a.m., but he didn't show up until ten after ten.

I was so relieved to see his smiling face as he got out of his car that I wrapped my arms around him enthusiastically, completely ignored his tardiness. Nate was never on time, and he had conditioned me to accept this minor flaw. It didn't occur to me that it was a warning sign he valued his time more than mine.

We checked into the hotel, a half-decent Garden Inn close to JFK Airport. His reason for not booking one in the center of the city, where I could check out his modeling work, was that he didn't want the bright lights and energy of New York City to overshadow our time together. He was craving one-on-one time in a more private setting. So was I.

We savored every moment of it. Immediately after checking into the hotel, Nate whisked me onto the freshly made bed. He sucked on my ears and neck like a starving man inhaling his first bite of food in weeks. His insatiable appetite for my body and early, vocal release reassured me that he must have been faithful since leaving Toronto.

I fought the thought of him cheating every time it tried to creep in, but I was secretly worried that he was at least tempted, being surrounded by models. When he described the photo shoots he was working on, a distinctly female name would pop up now and then. I played it cool, like I didn't notice. Of course he would be working with women; that was no reason to feel insecure.

After our first passionate explosion, we went for a short walk to a coffee shop for a quick lunch, before eagerly returning to the hotel for round two. This time, Nate lasted significantly longer and refused to let go of me once he was finished.

"I'm inside and wrapped around you. Now that I have you again, I'm never letting you go," he whispered in my ear while tightening his arms around my waist.

"It would be wonderful if we could stay like this forever."

"Why can't we?" His puppy dog eyes pleaded with me to consider his recurring invite.

"You know why we can't. Nate, can't we just enjoy this moment?" I didn't want to endure the same debate yet again, now that we were finally together.

Nate on the other hand, felt it was the perfect time. "Seriously, I need a girlfriend who I actually get to see. I don't think we can make it work unless you move out here. We can't waste money on a room every weekend and I need to be in New York." His limp penis shrunk from me as he rolled backwards, creating a gap between us.

"I want to see you too! I do. But school matters to me too. I can't just drop out," I tried to explain.

"So, are you saying I was wrong for dropping out?" His body language was clearly showing defensiveness.

"I'm not saying anything like that! You had a solid reason for dropping out. I don't."

"Okay, so what if I tell you that I found a reason for you to move here? A real job in fashion."

"What? Why didn't you say something earlier?" I questioned.

"I needed to know for sure that you'd want to live with me. I never know what you're thinking, and I need you to be committed to this relationship."

"Of course I'm committed. I love you." The words felt so natural.

"I love you too. Let's get a place together. I'm making good money. We can start looking this weekend." He pulled me in close and begun kissing me passionately.

"It's not like I can just move to another country," I softly pointed out.

"Why not?" Nate fired back.

"I would have to apply for a work visa and that takes time." A light bulb suddenly went off. "How were you able to get one so fast?"

"It doesn't work that way for modeling. I'm hired on an International contract through an agency. Plus, most of my jobs are cash anyway." His lack of hesitation and the confidence he displayed while explaining his ability to work in another country made it believable.

"I doubt they offer temporary visas for fashion designers."

"Tell them your plan is to go to school here. Isn't there a famous fashion school in New York?"

"Yes, I guess. It still won't happen quickly."

"I can wait if I know you're coming." Nate pulled me closer into his chest and softly sucked on my bottom lip before whispering, "you're worth the wait."

"So, tell me more about this job," I conceded.

"I will, but I want to save the surprise for over dinner."

Secure inside his arms, I agreed enthusiastically. Wrapped together again, we took a little afternoon nap before showering together and heading out to dinner. He took me to an upscale Jamaican restaurant, where he was greeted warmly—as if he was a regular. When he went to the washroom, I saw him chatting with a man who looked like he worked in the kitchen, so I asked.

"Have you been here before?"

"I've grabbed food here once or twice. Everything I tried so far was pretty good," Nate said.

"I've never tried Jamaican food, so you can order for me. Anything is good unless it has pork or beans in it. I like pretty much everything else."

"I love that you trust me enough to pick your meal. It's my honor." He smiled at me warmly.

"It looks like I'm also trusting you to pick my job. So, are you finally ready to tell me all about it?" I couldn't wait any longer.

"Have you heard of Century 21?"

"The department store?"

"Yes! The huge, historic, well-known Century 21 department store has an opening in their women's department, and I have a few connections there already."

"You've modelled for them?" I asked.

"Sort of... Anyway, it's only entry level, and the pay is not great, but I'll be making enough to cover the both of us," he continued.

"It's not really the kind of career I had in mind." It was hard to hide my disappointment, but retail sales has never interested me.

"You need to work your way up. It's a starting point, and you're ambitious. Isn't it worth a chance, so we can be together?" Nate's pleading eyes were piercing through my better judgment.

Luckily, our deeply personal, public discussion was interrupted by the waitress.

"Are you ready to order?"

"Yes, this is her first time trying Jamaican cuisine, so we'll split a few things for her to try. We'll start with an order of crab cakes, followed by a crispy chicken salad. Then we'll share a jerk chicken with fried plantains for dinner."

"Anything to drink?"

"Sure, two Red Stripes."

Nate ordered our meal with only a glance at the menu. Everything he picked was fine with me, except the plantains. I had no idea what they were, or whether I would like them. I also would have ordered something other than beer to drink, but I knew Red Stripe was the official Jamaican choice. I was less concerned with our dinner selection and more unsure of where this relationship was headed.

After the waitress left, Nate switched gears. "Have you ever tried real jerk chicken? This place has the best in New York City."

"I've tried it before, but never at a Jamaican restaurant."

"This place is known for it. I'm so happy I can finally share these experiences with you. Ever since the moment I arrived, I knew you were the only thing that was missing here."

My eyes welled with tears. I loved being with him; he always said the right thing. Suddenly the thought of working a retail position until I was able to climb the ladder sounded appealing. It was a step in the right direction, and it would be exciting to live in New York.

"The entire time you were gone, I was wishing I was with you," I responded.

"Then be with me. Take a chance on love, and be with me here in New York."

"Maybe it is possible. Maybe it's time I took a chance in life. I'm overdue for a rebellious adventure." His irresistible charm was wearing me down.

"Yes! Now that's the woman I love!" Nate exclaimed.

He got up from his seat to give me a quick squeeze and a soft peck on the cheek. The waitress was returning with our beers, so he sat back down mighty quick. My legs were vibrating under the table with adrenaline over what I had just agreed to do. My parents would not be pleased; hell, I wasn't even sure if *I* actually believed it was a wise move.

"I'd like to finish the semester, so it's not a waste of money. There's less than four weeks left, anyway," I offered as a compromise.

"Sure, I bet Tanya can make that work. She was looking for help during the holidays that could carry over into the new year. The place is huge, so there's lots of opportunities."

"Maybe we can visit tomorrow? I'd like to see what I'm agreeing to before we commit to a place," I suggested.

"I need to run into the city for an appointment, some potential work, so I can drop you off at Century 21. I'll come back for you after, and we'll check out what's for rent in the area. This is going to be perfect!" Nate seemed quite confident this was a solid plan, and I trusted him.

Even though everything was moving way too fast, I nodded yes enthusiastically. I had nothing else planned during our weekend visit, and it was worth looking into further. Nate was worth holding on to. I needed to explore all possibilities in life.

Everything I ate tasted pretty good, even the plantains. I wasn't as impressed with the jerked chicken as I thought I would be, since it didn't taste anything like the kind my uncle made. Of course, I told Nate that it was the best I had ever tried.

Our evening was capped off by our third vigorous round of love-making. The time apart made me crave his body. There was a part of me that could rationalize that experience was worth more than education. I didn't know sex would curl my toes and raise the hairs on the back of my neck, until Nate and I felt comfortable enough to enjoy each other with reckless abandon. It was through trial and error that we learned how to get the most from one another.

My mind began to rationalize this obviously irrational decision.

I already had more than a full and successful year of education, plus I'm a fast learner. Maybe freeing myself from the constraints of school would give me everything I needed to succeed. I was optimistic when Nate dropped me off at the department store the next day, shortly before lunch hour. I wandered around with that positive mindset and was mesmerized by the flurry of activity. Working here could be an exciting adventure.

The plan was for him to pick me up at 1:30 p.m., at the same entrance where he dropped me off. I went back a little early and grabbed a seat on the bench. I had picked us up iced coffees at the café just before leaving as a treat. My right leg was bouncing up and down with anticipation, so I rested the tray of drinks next to me. I was ready to take a major leap in life, and trusted Nate would catch me.

Around ten minutes before two o'clock, I began drinking my iced coffee. It was barely cold anymore and I didn't want it to spoil. It was an unseasonably warm day for late November. By two o'clock, my cup was empty and his was watered down by melted ice. I dumped both in the garbage a few feet from the bench, then began pacing along the sidewalk. I was going to trust my future to Nate and I couldn't even count on him to pick me up on time.

Nate didn't arrive until twenty after two and my annoyance with his constant tardiness was turning into worry about his whereabouts. I ended up feeling mainly grateful once I saw his smile, somehow the anger faded. I could tell he had a good reason for the delay by the massive grin on his face.

"I was beginning to worry. What happened to you?" I enquired as I hopped inside the passenger side.

"I'm so sorry, but I have amazing news. I found a place for us! Someone I was working with today is subletting a recently updated one bedroom for $1,250 a month, plus utilities. I think we can afford that." His eyes sparkled with excitement.

"Did you see it? Can I see it?" The wondrous possibilities of the moment and his boyish exuberance were igniting my enthusiasm.

"Yes, I just came from there. I wanted to make sure it wasn't a dump before I showed it to you. I can afford eight hundred dollars on my own, if you can come up with the other four hundred fifty and utilities. We'll make it work!"

His energy was contagious, and the place was as great as he made it out to be. It was small but clean, with updated appliances. It was only a fifteen-minute drive from the mall I was going to be working at, which was ideal. By the time we got back to the hotel, everything was in motion. The current tenant had given notice for January 1st, and we agreed to take over the lease. Before I left New York on Sunday, I had co-signed on an apartment with my boyfriend.

I don't normally make life-altering decisions without at least running it by my mother and Rachel. They know me better than anyone, and have always been valuable guiding lights. I was trying to predict their reaction on the flight back to Toronto. My stomach ached, knowing they would probably disapprove of such a drastic change in my plans.

Once I was back in our dorm, it took me three days to tell Kassie. She wasn't overly surprised, and quickly decided my impulsiveness could work in her favor. She wanted to move in with Dave; this gave her an opportunity to bring it up to him.

The following weekend, Nate confirmed that his friend would have a permanent job for me in the women's department, if I was willing to cover a few shifts over the Christmas holidays. She took care of arranging the interview for a temporary visa and all of the employment paperwork by email. It happened so fast that it wasn't sinking in.

I agreed to come in for training December 15th and 16th, then work December 22nd, 23rd, 24th, 28th, and 29th. It worked out to over forty hours, making it worth renting a hotel again. Nate was still crashing on a buddy's couch, so a hotel was the only option until our apartment was ready.

Strategic Separation

Working all of those hours meant I wouldn't be able to go home for the holidays. I knew in my heart that the news would not go over well with my parents. I was running out of time and had to fill them in on my plans, sooner rather than later.

Finally, on the 10th of December, I cautiously approached the subject with my mom. My heart was racing so fast I wondered if she could hear it through the phone. "I have some big and wonderful news, Mom, but I need you to hear me out."

"I've always heard you out. What's going on?"

"I can't come home for Christmas, because I just landed a real job in the fashion industry."

"Oh, honey, that's great! We understand. I know you're becoming a career woman and we're proud," she explained with sincere joy.

"Thank you, Mom." I exhaled upon hearing her initial supportiveness.

"Is it an apprenticeship through school?"

"No, it's not through school."

I opened my mouth to tell her more, but nothing came out. I feared it would break her heart, and I couldn't find the words on my own until I was actually forced to explain the reality of this job opportunity.

"So, tell me all about it! How did you get it?" my mom continued enquiring, out of genuine interest in me.

"Through a modeling friend of Nate's."

"What will you be doing?"

"Mostly sales and merchandising, but there's great opportunity for advancement."

"Where is it?" My relentless mother continued to pursue the details.

"A department store. They need me for the Christmas rush."

"So, you'll be a cashier?" she asked.

"It's more than just that, but that's part of it," I replied, as vaguely as possible.

"Do you have any time off around the holidays?"

"I work through the twenty-fourth, and then again on the twenty-eighth. It would be a long drive home in between," I replied, completely leaving out the fact that I would be coming from New York rather than Toronto. My parents didn't know that Nate was officially living in New York, so I certainly wasn't ready to tell them about me moving there.

"Let me talk to your dad; maybe we can cover a flight home as part of your present. I'd really love to see you at Christmas. I miss you."

"I miss you too, Mom." After a brief silence, I added, "I need to go, Mom, but we'll talk soon. Love you."

"I love you too."

I gave Rachel about the same details the following night, although she prodded significantly more aggressively than my mother. I left out the part about quitting school, moving to New York and living with Nate. She's more understanding than my mom, because she knows how much this relationship means to me. However, she's a straight-shooter. She wouldn't beat around the bush if she didn't think it was a good idea. I wasn't ready to listen to anyone else's opinion.

I had a strong suspicion that my family and Rachel wouldn't be impressed by the job offer if they knew it meant quitting school. However, I wasn't able to avoid the subject for very long, because my mom called two days later with a plan to ensure I was home for the holidays.

"There's a flight to Windsor out of Pearson airport at 10:20 p.m. on the 24th. We will pay for it and your return on the 27th. This way you don't miss Christmas Day with us. We want you home."

Silence for seconds that felt like minutes, as I debated my rebuttal. I was desperately wishing I hadn't answered the phone. What excuse could I give to turn down this offer that wouldn't break her heart?

"Mom, it's just too rushed. I have things to do here."

"Come on, Katie, please! Christmas dinner won't be the same without you." Her words pierced through me like a knife. "What else are you going to do on Christmas day?"

"Fine! I'll come home, but I have to tell you something that you might not like." I had to start the conversation somehow, and my parents always insisted that honesty was the best policy.

"If it's about that boy, I guess he can come to dinner if it's important to you," she interrupted.

"Thanks, he is important to me, but I'm not sure yet about his holiday plans." I paused long enough for her to jump in.

"You can always talk to me. What's going on?" my mother interjected in her most motherly voice.

"I won't be in Toronto. The job is in New York," I blurted, with as much confidence as I could manage.

"New York? How are you going to work in New York? Is it temporary?"

"I'm moving to New York." I dropped the bomb with a steady voice and trembling hands.

"When? How can you afford to live in New York? What about your schooling? Where is this job?" My mom stammered question after question, not giving me long enough to answer any of them in between. Her shock resonated through the phone.

"Mom, I know this sounds sudden, but I've been thinking about it for awhile. Nate is getting real work experience in New York. I miss him, and want to do the same."

"Nate!" she snorted loudly, her soft demeanor fading quickly.

"Listen, I'm an adult, and I can cover my expenses. This is important to me."

"School used to be important to you," she argued.

"Fashion is what I love, and Nate. This plan gives me both."

She sighed loudly before conceding. "Can you at least come home at Christmas, so we can discuss this properly? We'll fly you home from New York. I don't care what it costs; I want you home."

I agreed after a short debate, knowing I currently had too many other things to stress over. I was falling behind in my course work and not as prepared for finals as I had hoped. I was nervous about working in New York, moving in with Nate, and now, seeing my family at Christmas. My mind was constantly racing, and the chaos began to consume me.

I was so disorganized that I forgot to book my flight and had to pay a higher rate for a crappier flight to New York on the 14th. When I arrived, we had a more routine session of love-making and I insisted on going straight to bed afterwards. There were less than six hours until my first shift at Century 21 department store.

I felt the role was worth putting extra effort into my appearance, so I woke up over an hour before it was time to leave for work. Nate kept tugging at my body, trying to entice me back into bed, but I was focused.

I primped until I looked like I belonged in the New York fashion world. I was wearing fitted black dress pants with a sleeveless, lace collared, cream-colored blouse that I'd splurged on last year at a local designer's boutique in the Distillery District. I only wore it on special occasions, and this certainly qualified. It looked sophisticated under my burgundy leather long jacket with the faux-fur lining.

Nate and I arrived fifteen minutes early, as I requested, but their human resource manager wasn't there until quarter after nine. Nate was getting antsy before it was even nine o'clock, and he had run out of patience by the time Karen showed up.

"Karen, is it?" he asked as she was approaching us in the lobby.

"Yes. Nate and Katelyn, right?"

"Yes, I'm sure you can guess who's who...and I'm running late, so I hope everything works out for both of you. I'll be sure to tell Tanya how grateful I am that you are giving this lovely lady the chance to work here," he quickly announced, before pecking awkwardly at my cheek and taking off.

"Hi, I'm Katelyn. It's a pleasure to meet you," I said, extending my hand toward the much shorter woman.

"Nice to meet you too. Have you worked in retail before?" she replied, completely ignoring my hand directly in front of her.

"I have customer service experience through waitressing, and I studied fashion in Toronto. I'm excited to learn more."

"Can you work a POS system?" she asked, without looking up from her cellphone screen.

"I have used various versions at different restaurants and pick up any computer software fairly quickly."

"Okay, I'm going to introduce you to Gina, our women's department manager. She can teach you the ropes and find some work for you to do. It's good to dive right into things this weekend, because it will be a zoo for the next two weeks. Stop by my office on the second floor at break, so we can fill in the rest of your paperwork."

"Thank you. I will," I said before following her through a maze of different departments. The store was neatly organized and ready for the rush of customers who had started to flood in. Gina was helping one of them when we approached. Karen waited silently two feet behind Gina, allowing her to finish dealing with the customer before getting her attention.

"Gina, would you come here for a moment?" Karen called in her direction.

Gina hopped over enthusiastically before Karen could even finish the request. "Hello Karen, good morning. What may I help you with today?"

"This is Katelyn, a new trainee. I need you to show her around the department. Let her shadow someone in customer service in the morning, and then a replenisher in the afternoon. Please send me an email letting me know the scope of the training at the end of the day." Each word was pronounced precisely. I was beginning to see why Karen had such an impressive role at what I was guessing to be a fairly young age.

"Hello, so nice to meet you." I extended my hand in her direction, but Gina didn't notice; her eyes were fixated on Karen. Apparently handshakes aren't customary in New York.

"Hello." Gina gave me a quick glance before responding to what was obviously her superior. "Of course you can rely on me, Karen. I will have a full detailed report of what we accomplish today and what still needs to be worked on before I leave for the night."

"Thank you. I know she's in good hands. Please make the most of this day, ladies." And away she went.

Gina finally turned her attention toward me, scanning me up and down as if she was sizing me up for a fight. "Your outfit is fine for today, but it's strongly recommended that you wear clothing from our store. The expectation is that you always look and act professional at any time when you're representing the Century 21 brand. That includes time inside the store before or after you start your shift. There's quite a bit that we need you to learn today. Do you have something you can use to take notes?"

"Yes, I have a notebook in my purse," I quickly responded, while scrambling to retrieve it without dumping the contents on the floor. My hands were trembling ever-so-slightly.

"Okay, I need to make my rounds, so keep up and make sure you can hear me. This will help you see how I want my department to run." She whipped around and begun weaving her way through countless racks and shelving.

Her driven gait was exceptionally fast, but I had no trouble keeping up. She finally stopped at a section that carried purses, belts, and other fashion accessories. A petite blonde was standing behind a sales desk a few feet away.

"Audrey, please come here," Gina called in her direction. The tiny women walked over to us with an overeager smile.

"Yes, Gina." Her voice was meek and quiet.

"These racks are disorganized. It looks sloppy. I want these sorted into one rack of large crossbody and long shoulder strap bags, one for medium sized purses and day bags, and a third for evening bags and clutches. I'd like to see that done by the next time I'm back in this area." Gina's instructions inspired a structured nod, followed by immediate action.

I scanned the rows of bags and, for the most part, they were already sorted by size and style. A few bags in the front had been misplaced, most likely by customers, but most were already grouped with similar styles.

Without any commentary toward me, Gina continued on her warpath. She found something to nitpick in each employee's designated area, and every employee was quick to respond to her requests. She didn't acknowledge me again until she made it back to the entranceway to the department.

"Did our walk-through clearly demonstrate the standards I expect to be maintained in my department?" she asked in a tone a prosecutor would use to cross examine the defendant.

"Yes. I understand the importance of making a good first impression on the customer and how necessary it is to keep every section properly organized," I eagerly responded in an obedient manner. I needed this job to work out.

"Were you paying enough attention to go around and ensure all the issues I pointed out have been corrected?" she continued.

"Yes, I believe I could do that quite successfully. I took detailed notes on your instructions for each area." My studious ways were about to be tested.

"Okay, that's what I want you to do. Make your way back through the departments and make sure everything I pointed out has been fixed. Can you do that? And this time, just say yes. I don't have time for your ass-kissing fluff." Gina's words kept poking at the bubble I so desperately didn't want to burst.

"Yes," I said as flat and emotionless as possible, trying not to be discouraged by her brutal brevity. The moment the word slipped from my mouth, she was gone. I retraced our steps, sheepishly checking every rack to see if the other six employees had done what she asked. Everything looked close enough to perfect, but I still tidied up a few things along the way. I had a feeling that Gina wouldn't be satisfied with "good enough."

It took me a bit to locate Gina after I was finished my inspection. Her office was tucked into an alcove between two tall shelves of shoes, at the very back of the store. I should have asked another employee, but the combination of not being properly introduced to anyone and then checking up on their work made me feel so uncomfortable that I didn't say a word to anyone as I looped through the store for a second time this morning.

I gently tapped on the door frame to her room, since it was wide open. "Hi, Gina."

"Yes?" She responded without looking up from her computer.

"I went back through the store, double-checked the things you wanted done, and believe everything has been addressed."

"Are you certain I won't find anything out of place?" she asked with one eyebrow raised dramatically.

"Well, everything was done. I can't guarantee customers in the store haven't moved things since I passed by."

"Then double-check it again until you can be certain." Her voice was steady and direct.

My mind was racing for an appropriate response. I could never assure every section was in perfect order as long as there were customers in the store. I couldn't physically see the entire women's department from any one spot in the building.

"I'm certain it was organized when I walked through it. The store is wonderfully busy and I worry customers might misplace something."

"Then you should be outside, in the store, looking for it. That way you can put things back where they belong as soon as they are misplaced."

"Oh, sure. Of course, I can do that." I stood still for a moment, waiting for her reply before realizing that our conversation had concluded in her eyes. I wandered back into the store, searching for things that were out of place that I could put back. At the same time, I was trying to develop an impression of the other employees, hoping to make a connection. My first day wasn't starting like I hoped.

My day continued in a similar fashion, except that she asked me to put away stock and shadow cashiers for the afternoon. Although no one made much of an effort to make me feel welcomed, at least it gave me the chance to introduce myself to my co-workers. When Nate picked me up precisely at 7:00 p.m. (thankfully on time), I was dreading the thought of returning the following day.

"How was it, baby? Did you wow them?" He sounded as hopeful as a kid on Christmas morning.

"Not exactly. I'm not sure this is the right job for me," I confessed, looking out the passenger window.

"Of course it is! You're working in the heart of New York fashion. You can't judge it based on the first day."

"It was a pretty dismal first day," I confessed.

"What's the worst thing that happened?"

I scanned my recollection for some significant event that justified my disappointment in the position. Instead of answering him, I went over the day in my head and rationalized that it was a typical first day at any large company. They may not have done anything to make me feel overly welcomed, but no one said anything that should make me feel like I wasn't.

"Well, sweetheart? What was so bad about it?" he pressed.

"I guess it wasn't that bad, just disappointing. I didn't feel welcome or needed. I spent most of the day in silence, just watching people work."

"That's how you'll learn how to do it. Just give it some time. You'll make friends fast." My sweet man did his best to reassure me.

Nate made sense; I was overreacting. I was risking my original career plan for this venture, and my nerves were getting the best of me. My second day of training was similar, but I consciously made the best of it. I engaged more with my co-workers, making small talk by asking each one of them how long they had worked there, and what did they do for fun.

Four out of six were eager to talk, and the other two at least answered the questions with a smile. It was a great way to break the ice, while giving me more insight into the work environment. Out of the six employees, Eudora had worked there the longest, with four years of experience. Audrey, Kim, and Sarah all had somewhere between one and two years of experience at the store. Dana had only been there for three months, and Louise had started the week before.

Eudora gave me the briefest responses to my inquiry. "This is my fourth Christmas season."

"Do you like working here?"

"I guess...enough to stay four years."

"What do you like to do for fun?"

"Lots of stuff, outside of here." She gave me a puffy cheeked smile before turning her back to me to scan an aisle for items out of place. I tried talking to her later on and only received polite nods and smiles in return. I overheard her interacting with customers and her demeanor appeared genuinely kind.

Kim was almost as quiet, especially when it came to discussing work. "I was hired last November, so this is my second year working the Christmas chaos."

"Do you like it here?"

"Sure," she replied, without making eye contact. Her focus was on carefully checking the shoe racks to make sure they were organized neatly by size and style.

"What do you do for fun?"

"Dance, run, sing, party. Pretty much whatever I want after work is over."

She was slowly moving herself away from me as we chatted. Her last reply was barely audible as she rounded the corner to inspect the row containing size six women's dress shoes and boots. I didn't follow her.

The other four women, ranging from nineteen to twenty-eight, chatted my ear off and asked me quite a few questions about myself and my reasons for moving here. They thought it was cool that I was from Canada, and begun calling me "Miss Canuck." I left my shift on the 16th feeling hopeful that it wouldn't be long before I had some real New York friends. Nate was relieved by my change of heart when he drove me to the airport.

"I was so worried after yesterday. I was scared you'd be leaving today and not have any reason to come back."

"You're enough of a reason for me to want to come back. You make it worth it. The job will do for now, but there's always a reason to be in New York if you're living here." I meant every word.

Nate lifted me off the ground and begun kissing me passionately, just inside the entrance of the airport. I had a goofy grin on my face the entire plane ride, counting down the days until I would be returning to see him.

I spent the next week brainstorming ideas to market and improve Century 21, so I could show Gina that I was more ambitious than the rest. I also decided to pack the rest of my belongings, which didn't leave nearly enough time for studying. I had high enough marks that there was no threat of not passing my courses. I figured my overall grade was irrelevant, now that I was already working in the industry.

I was committed to devoting just as much passion and energy into my new role as I had with my education, but I didn't want to come on too strong the first week of work. My second weekend leading to up Christmas was mainly spent organizing and replenishing floor displays. A few times a day, I was called to help out at the cash register when the lines were backed up. I was only called if everyone else was already serving customers. It was good experience, plus I had the pleasure of Nate waiting for me outside as soon as I finished.

I tried to convince him to go home with me for Christmas, but he didn't even want to entertain the idea. His mom's new boyfriend was treating her to a luxury cruise for the holidays, and he had no family to visit. I offered him the possibility of staying with my family (secretly hoping they'd agree), but Nate didn't even want me to ask them. There was always the chance that new work would pop up. He was a fresh young face, and suddenly in high demand.

My father picked me up at the Windsor airport and after asking about my flight, he was relatively quiet. That's normal for him, and it was a less than twenty-minute drive home. It was almost midnight on Christmas Eve, and the house was as silent as the car ride had been. We gave each other a hug good-night and retired to our rooms.

For the first time, sleeping in my teenage bed felt awkward. I no longer viewed myself as David and Joanne's daughter, but as an independent woman who was building a life of her own. I was determined to spend the next few days proving to my parents that I was a mature enough to make this major life decision.

Christmas morning brought me back to my childhood in the best way. We were all there, laughing, exchanging thoughtful gifts. I had bought my sisters each a trendy, New York style outfit from Century 21 that they both ran upstairs to immediately try on. I'm a pro at buying clothes for other people. I gave my parents a $100 gift card to the Keg in Windsor that I'd picked up when I was home at Thanksgiving.

I was spoiled with clothes, new bedding, a better blow dryer, and two sets of shelves from my parents. Amy bought me a long, silver necklace with set of matching earrings. Tina gave me a gift card to Old Navy, so we could use it on our traditional Boxing Day shopping spree. It was the only store all three of us agreed on.

Christmas was spent visiting family, stuffing ourselves with turkey and general good cheer. No one brought up Nate or me moving to New York. I certainly wasn't willing to introduce the subject, and thought I might escape any unpleasant conversation up until our annual trip to the mall. My mom and sisters were parked in front of Devonshire Mall just before it opened, waiting to take advantage of the after-holiday sales, when my visit took a sour turn.

"I'm going to Bowerings. I need to start collecting stuff for when I buy a house," Amy advised the rest of the car.

"Great idea! I'm not sure Nate and I have everything we need yet. He hardly has anything for the kitchen," I added. My mother sighed loudly and the car went silent for a few minutes.

"Let's go to Old Navy first. I need new shirts for practice." Tina broke the silence.

"Sounds good. I can use my gift card to buy some new dress pants to wear to work."

More silence. No one said anything again until 7:00 a.m., when the mall opened its doors to all the early bird shoppers. Amy yelled, "It's go time!" and we exited my mom's SUV with giddy enthusiasm. We went to Old Navy first and worked our way around the mall, stocking up on clothes, accessories, and a few kitchen gadgets. I also bought a new bra and some sexy lingerie. My mom couldn't contain her disapproval any longer.

"I'm pretty sure Nate will appreciate this purchase." I held it up to show it off.

"Can we go the rest of the day without hearing his name?" My mom couldn't contain her disapproval any longer. She rolled her eyes as her snappy response cut through my cheerful mood.

"Why can't I talk about him? That's the man I love. I should be able to say his name without getting attitude from you." My tone quickly switched to one of defensive frustration as I shoved the lace undergarment back into my shopping bag.

"We can talk about him later. I would like a nice day with my girls, without any drama. Can we agree on that?" Mom pleaded, in a noticeably kinder tone.

"How is it drama if all I'm doing is mentioning my boyfriend's name?" I asked, stubborn and unwilling to drop the subject.

"Honestly, I don't trust your boyfriend. People around here talk, and I haven't heard one good thing about him since you left. I think you're making a big mistake," my mother responded bluntly.

"Other people don't know him like I do. You don't know him! It's my life, and you should trust me!" I didn't wait for her to answer. I stormed away, swing my shopping bags like a madwoman. No one in my family followed me.

I called Rachel to see if she was home and then a taxi service to drive me to her and Chris's apartment. I was fuming. I could feel my heart pounding rapidly in my chest. My mom loved Nate the first time she met him. Her change of heart was based on unfounded rumors. It wasn't fair to him, or to me.

After a quick squeeze hello, I repeated the heated exchange with my mother to Rachel. She nodded sympathetically—and then took my mom's side: "She's only concerned because she wants what's best for you."

"He *is* what's best for me. Nate makes me happier than I thought possible. Why can't she see that?" Unexpected tears rolled down my cheeks, prompting Rachel to give me another, significantly longer, hug.

When she released me from her embrace, she tactfully changed the subject. We spent the next hour catching up on each other's daily lives. My emotions settled down just as my stomach began to rumble. I had been planning to go to our favorite all-you-can-eat Chinese buffet after shopping with my mom and sisters.

"I'm starving, and I was supposed to go with them to Ming Wah's for lunch. Now I'm craving Chinese."

"You can still go and meet them, right? They may still be there. They love you, and you can make peace before you leave," Rachel sweetly suggested.

I sent Amy a text to see if they were still at the restaurant. I got a simple *yes* in return, so I advised her that Rachel and I were on our way to join them. I hoped that having Rachel with me would stop my mom from discussing the earlier incident. I was leaving for New York in less than twenty-four hours. I didn't want to spend that time arguing with my mom.

The only negativity happened the moment I walked in the door, when I asked why they were still there. We had almost been done shopping when I left, which was over an hour before. Tina explained that they had split up to search the mall for me prior to leaving, because they didn't want to leave me stranded. I humbly apologize and the focus shifted to Rachel.

My mom and sisters were excited to see Rachel. They hadn't seen her in months, so the first few minutes were spent fussing over her. When the small talk trailed off, we both excused ourselves to fill our plates. Lunch was pleasant enough, and our girl time continued afterwards in my parents' kitchen. Rachel drove me there and stayed with us until it was time to make dinner.

Under Attack

I falsely assumed the attack on Nate was over. While we were cutting vegetables and swapping comical childhood stories, every exchange felt comfortable and fluid. There was no awkwardness or attitude, which is probably why I let my guard down. We were clearing the table and it made me think of a sweet story about Nate.

"We've been ordering takeout a lot, because we're staying in a hotel until our apartment is ready. Nate started washing the plastic utensils and calling them our 'starter set' for when we get our place." I laughed, hoping someone else would as well. Silence... After a few seconds, I pushed my luck and continued.

"I've already packed my set of silverware; he knows it. He's just being silly. After we eat, he grabs all the garbage and says, 'Allow me to do the dishes, my lady,' then throws out everything except the plastic forks. He washes them in the bathroom sink and lays them out on a Kleenex to dry. He's always trying to make me laugh."

As I rambled, I scanned my family's faces for their reaction. No one made eye contact. The tension rose so fast and thick that I felt like it was suffocating me. I wanted to force a response, so after a short pause, I added, "I'm so lucky to be with him."

"Amy, Tina, can you finish up in here, please?" My mom asked my sisters calmly. As they nodded, she turned to me and said, "Let's go in the living room and have a good chat about your plans."

Somehow, my father was already waiting for us with the TV off. He shifted back and forth in his chair as if he was uncomfortable, almost agitated. My mom's face was scrunched up in pain, like she was fighting one of her terrible migraines. I was feeling a combination of nervousness and frustration. It was heartbreaking that they couldn't just be happy for me.

"Katelyn, you know our concern over this huge life decision is because we love you. Right?" my mom began.

"Of course. I love you both."

"You're quitting school, moving to a different country, and living with a boy you barely know. That doesn't seem like a well-thought-out decision," my mom continued.

"Nate and I have been together for over a year. I know him better than I know anyone else. I put a lot of thought into this decision. I'm doing what's best for me!" I argued loudly.

"You moving to New York is what's best for Nate. Staying in school would be what's best for you," my dad chimed in firmly, looking at my mom rather than me.

"Being with him is what's best for me!" I yelled back.

"Since when do you put a man ahead of your own goals?" Amy, who had been eavesdropping from the kitchen, stormed into the conversation.

"I want to work in fashion, and we'll be living in the fashion capital of the world. I have a job in the fashion industry. This is exciting, and I would like some support."

"You're a cashier at a department store. That's customer service, not fashion," Amy bit back.

I jumped up from the couch, debating whether to grab my shoes and run outside or grab Amy by the hair and toss her to the floor. Before I could decide, my father grabbed my wrist gently, but firmly enough to keep me planted.

"Why can't you guys be happy for me?" I pleaded, tears welling in my eyes.

"We don't think you know the real Nathan. People who grew up with him are convinced he's guilty of what happened to that girl. The police have no other suspects. Has he ever been violent with you?" mom asked calmly, as dad's grip on my wrist tightened.

"No!" I shouted. "He has never shown any signs of violence or anger. He was interviewed by police, and they confirmed his innocence. Why won't you let this go?"

"He doesn't seem willing to be interviewed by the Windsor police. Why doesn't he come home?" my father added.

"He's working a lot right now, and makes great money doing it. Nate has his priorities straight. He wants to make as much money as he can while he's still the hot new thing, because he knows he can't live off his looks forever." I vehemently defended my man.

My dad laughed and my mom rolled her eyes, which made my blood boil and my body shake. I yanked my arm from my dad's grip and bolted to my bedroom, slamming the door behind me. I began shoving everything I had into my suitcase. I was crying so hard that my vision was too blurry to call Rachel. Instead, I dove into bed, pulling the covers far over my head. Even though it was still hours before I'd normally go to bed, I fell asleep, dreaming of being back with Nate in New York.

My flight out of Windsor was at 10:50 a.m., so I stayed in my room until 8:30. I went downstairs, placed my suitcase by the door, and approached the table where my dad, mom and Tina were eating. Amy was either avoiding me or working.

"Are you still driving me to the airport?" I asked, looking only at my dad.

"I can, but I'd rather drive you to Toronto." His smug response reignited my rage from the night before. I was a grown woman and my parents had no right to stop me.

"Fucking forget it!" I snapped back. I turned my back on my family and made my way outside, slowing only to slide into my shoes and pick up my purse and suitcase. Once outside, I called a taxi to drive me to the airport.

Truthfully, I expected my mom, or at least Tina, to come outside and apologize before I went. My mom never wants us to part on bad terms, and will make a point of resolving any differences as quickly as possible. It took ten minutes for my ride to arrive, and no one came outside to see me off.

It was a long, emotionally-draining flight home as I went over the last few days in my head. I should have stayed in New York with Nate. That was the worst Christmas I had experienced in my life up to that point, although I almost didn't make it to the following Christmas.

Nate greeted me at the airport with a bouquet of tropical flowers. He scooped me into his arms, only pulling away far enough to kiss me. I decided not to fill him in on the nastier details from my visit, saying only that they weren't thrilled I was dropping out of school.

"Let's just say my trip home wasn't the happy holidays I remember as a kid."

"That's okay. Your home is with me now, and we're going to be very happy." Nate gently rubbed my back, relieving all of my anger and family frustrations. "Are you hungry? We should grab something to eat on our ride back to the hotel, because once we get there, I'm going to spend the rest of the night showing you just how much you were missed."

Nate followed through on that promise. We grabbed a ready-made pizza and garlic bread en route, which neither of us touched until much later. As soon as we got off the elevator, he teased, "Hold onto that pizza with your life." He wrapped his arms around my waist, launching me up in the air and onto his shoulder. He carried me like a caveman into the hotel room, pulling the pizza box from my hand and dropping it onto the end table.

He then gently tossed me onto the plush hotel bed. His mouth eagerly explored every inch of me, before he finally thrust himself deep inside me. I moaned in approval. We spent the rest of the night rotating between ravishing each other's bodies and snacking on cold, greasy pizza.

The next few days flew by, as we were both busy working and preparing for our new home. It cost me almost $200 to ship the last of my belongings to our new place, which was at least cheaper than flying back to pick them up. Luckily, I was able to sell the little furniture I owned to other students before I started working at Century 21. I gave the money I made to Nate, so he could use it toward furniture for our new apartment. A large, soft bed was our top priority.

We picked up the keys to the apartment after work on New Year's Eve and spent the next few hours organizing everything. We were both giddy with excitement. Nate couldn't stop kissing and thanking me.

"I'm so happy we'll be living together. We're home, baby!" His enthusiasm was contagious.

"If my parents saw how happy you make me, they would understand why I needed to move to New York," I said, beaming at him.

"I'm guessing they weren't exactly thrilled when you told them."

"They were completely against the idea, especially dropping out of school," I replied, lying since their real angst was focused on Nate.

"Does what they say really matter?" Nate asked, giving me a look he knew I couldn't resist.

"I guess not, but I still wish they could be happy for us."

"You're an adult. Your parents' approval shouldn't matter," he insisted.

"Yeah, that's true," I muttered quietly.

"Fuck them, Kate. We're about to start our lives together. That's all that matters." His bold stance was followed by whisking me off my feet and testing out the new bed he ordered for us. It wasn't as soft as I'd hoped, but it held me in place while I rode him with wild abandon.

After we finished christening our new digs, Nate went out to pick up beer and Chinese takeout, so that we could ring in the New Year with a feast. It must have been hard to find a place that wasn't busy, because nearly two hours passed before he returned. There were less than twenty minutes left until the ball dropped at midnight.

We each cracked a beer and began stuffing our bellies. It was our second New Year's Eve together, of what I hoped would be many more. We fell asleep pressed up against each other, underneath my old comforter. Since it was a holiday, we had the entire day to do whatever we wanted. Of course, we slept until almost noon on New Year's Day.

For our first makeshift brunch in our new place, we heated up leftover Chinese food with scrambled eggs. After we ate, we decided to tour the area and see what was open. We were hoping to find a quaint pub where we could hang out and get to know the locals, but the only things we saw open were fast food joints and cheesy chain restaurants.

We drove around for over an hour before settling on a few beers and fried appetizers at an almost-empty Applebee's. We didn't even stay there a full hour, since both of us were focused more on the TV in the corner than each other. Although we normally are able to enjoy a comfortable silence with each other, it felt more awkward when were not conversing in public.

When we got back to the apartment, Nate went to lie down for a nap. I did a little more cleaning and organizing before settling down to watch TV. I kept the volume low, since our bedroom was only one thin wall away. The apartment was so small that it could fit inside my parent's front room.

I finally decided to join Nate shortly after nine o'clock, since the last few days had been physically exhausting and fairly emotional. Nate was on his cell phone when I walked in, although he was just ending his call.

"For sure, man, I'm on my way." I heard him say just as he noticed me walking in.

"You're going somewhere?"

"That was this guy Tom who owes me money. I was in some muscle shots for a new health-food store he's marketing. It was a small job, but it paid two hundred dollars. He has the cash now."

"Why don't you get it tomorrow? It's kind of late."

"It's like nine o'clock, Katie-Bear. That's only late in New York if you're a senior citizen. You get some sleep, and I'll be right back."

"I could go with you," I offered sincerely.

"No need." He gave me a quick kiss, slipped on his shoes and flew out the door before I could even respond.

It was well after midnight before he returned. I was tossing and turning, unable to sleep without him. I sat straight up when he opened the door to our room.

"What are you doing up?" Nate asked.

"What took you so long?" I was unable to hide my frustration.

"Oh, come on! Don't tell me you're going to be one of those jealous chicks who needs to know my every move!" Nate loudly snapped back. His words sounded slurred and bitter, far from the smitten man he'd seemed to be only a few hours prior.

"No, it's just a lot longer than you said you'd be."

"I lost track of time. Why does it matter?" His tense brows and squinty eyes exposed his aggravation.

"You *always* 'lose track of time!'" I snapped at him, unwilling to accept yet another excuse. I uprooted my entire life for him; all I was asking from him was to be on time or call if he was going to be late.

"Tom has more work for me. We were figuring out a schedule for a few projects. This is how I make a living, and the reason we're able to live in New York!" he snapped right back. I slunk back under the blanket, feeling foolish and insecure.

"Sorry, I was worried." I meekly apologized.

"Well, stop worrying."

"I'll try," I quietly mumbled.

Nate said, "Whatever," nodded, and jumped in the shower. Then he went to the couch, where he stayed until almost 3:00 a.m. I was still struggling to fall asleep and panicking about how tired I would be at work the next day. Sometime after he slipped in the bed beside me, I must have drifted off, because the next thing I heard was the alarm clock.

Nate was back to his adoring self by morning, and we had a quickie before he dropped me off at work. His day was going to be busy, so we decided I would walk home and pick up something for dinner at a market along the way. He would get home as soon as he could.

My work day dragged on. Gina was in a particularly bad mood and was harping on everyone in the department. I kept as busy as I could, but the store had significantly less traffic than the pre-holiday rush. The only busy area was the returns, so I volunteered to put away all the gifts people didn't actually want.

Being on your feet all day is tiring. Although I'm a lifelong runner and still fairly fit, my endurance was waning. I hadn't run in several weeks, or made any time for my yoga workout routine. I was slacking, and I felt sluggish. The walk was supposed to give me the energy boost I needed, but my feet were too sore to appreciate it.

I stopped at the first market I saw, just in case there wasn't another. I picked up carrots, mushrooms, lettuce, tomatoes, ranch salad dressing, mayonnaise, shredded cheese, eggs, bacon, ground turkey, bread, pasta sauce, Ritz crackers, two cans of chicken noodle soup, and a bag of penne noodles. I bought two new reusable grocery bags from the store to carry everything home in securely. I had never grocery shopped for us before and wasn't too sure what Nate would want to eat. We were so used to eating fast food.

I was wearing gloves. However, I'd chosen them based on how dainty they made my hands look, rather than their ability to keep my fingers warm. The temperature was below freezing and a light snowfall had begun to sprinkle the sky. Although it looked peaceful and magical, my fingertips went numb around the heavy bags within minutes of leaving the store. I still had a few miles to go, and my toes were losing feeling.

It took me over thirty minutes to walk home from the market. I dropped the bags on the kitchen counter, took a long, hot shower, and freshened up. I then spent twenty minutes on the couch with my aching feet resting on our cheap Ikea coffee table.

It was almost seven o'clock by the time I had the energy to make dinner. I filled our only saucepan with water and put it on the stove to boil for the pasta. I had just taken out a frying pan for the ground turkey when I heard the apartment door open. Nate walked in with a big smile on his face and a box of chocolates in his hand.

"Hello, my love. I brought you a sweet treat. I was in a good mood all day because I knew I was coming home to you." I eagerly extended my arms around him and gave him a lasting kiss that made my body tingle. He pulled me in closer, and I could feel him rise with arousal. I ground myself into him.

He lowered his hands to grab my firm ass, lifting me up so I could wrap my legs around his waist. Nate gently tossed me on the bed before groping every inch of me like a horny teenager. He softly bit my breast as his hard penis penetrated my pulsating body. I was shaking with anticipation. It didn't take long for Nate to explode inside me, which was good since the water was still boiling on the stove.

"Thanks for dessert, now what's for dinner?" Nate asked as he quickly redressed himself.

"I'm making spaghetti and salad. Is that all right?"

"Sure, as long as it's quick. I hate to say it, but I have a high-paying gig tonight."

"When? You just got home."

"It starts at 9:00 p.m., but I need to leave shortly after eight to make sure I get there on time. We need the money," he reasoned.

"What kind of gig would be so late at night?" I innocently enquired.

"It's a runway job for a new designer. Like a pop-up shop. It pays two hundred forty dollars for three hours of work. We can't pass that up. I'm doing this for us, remember?"

"Can I come with you? I'd love to see you work. Please?" I begged with my most adorable pout.

"No. It's still a job," he said in all seriousness.

"No one would need to know I was there to see you. I'll just check out the show."

"No, I'd be uncomfortable if I knew you were there watching me. I need to be focused."

"What's the name of the designer?" We rarely talked about his work and I wanted to know more about how he was spending his time.

"What's with the twenty-one questions? Is this an interrogation?" Nate shot back.

"No, of course not." I retreated reluctantly.

"It sounds like you don't trust me. What have I ever done for you to mistrust me?"

"Nothing, I'm sorry. I was just curious about your career. It's impressive, dating a model."

"I would say we are more than dating," Nate replied suggestively, pulling me in for a kiss.

"How about live-in lovers?" I flirted back.

"How about the love of my life?" he answered, before tilting me back for a passionate kiss.

"I love you, so of course, I want to be a part of your life in every way I can. But I understand why you don't want me there," I conceded, once our mouths finally separated.

"Thanks, love. It's just work. You know I can't pass up any opportunities at this point. Anyway, I'm doing all of this for us. That awesome welcome-home sex has left me starving for something a bit meatier. Let's eat," Nate said, as he walked the five steps from the bedroom to our tiny kitchen.

"It will take about twenty minutes. I just started making it."

"Why didn't you start dinner when you got home?"

"I was cold from the walk and needed a hot shower."

"Still, you should have been home for over an hour." Nate started scanning the apartment for evidence of how I spent that time.

"It took awhile to get home and I put my feet up for a few minutes." I thought about pointing out that he wasn't acting like he trusted me either, but things were already heated enough. I made the right decision, because he quickly softened his questioning.

"All right, I'll help you cook so we're not racing through our dinner time together. What can I do?" he offered.

"Great! I'll put the pasta on and make the salad, if you can start frying the turkey," I said cheerily, glad we had recovered from what could have been an ugly fight. I sincerely wanted our relationship and living situation to work out.

We made a great team and were able to finish making dinner in less than twenty minutes. Our teamwork gave us fifteen minutes sitting next to each other, eating our meal off the coffee table. Nate said he was saving the pay from these cash jobs to buy a little table and two chairs for us, even though we both agreed there was really no room for them in the apartment.

Our New Routine

Eventually, we settled into our new routine of playing house and working for a living. Due to the unpredictable hours Nate worked, we didn't get to spend as much time together as I would have hoped. And when we were home at the same time, we were either eating, sleeping, or making love.

If our living together was going to work, I needed to trust Nate—even when he came home from work several hours after I was expecting him. It certainly helped that he would usually bring home fresh donuts or Chinese takeout as his way of apologizing for being gone so long. A few times, he left $50 on the counter with a note, telling me to buy myself something pretty.

Although the situation wasn't ideal, Nate made me feel special and wanted. He was always excited to see me, and I blindly trusted him. I viewed our situation as making sacrifices now, so that we could have the best possible future together. In order to not resent him for letting me spend so much time alone, I decided it was time to create my own social life.

Ordinarily, I'd go for a walk or run to get to know my new surroundings better and hopefully make new friends. That's what I did when I moved to LaSalle and Toronto. Since I was standing on my feet all day at the store and then walking home after work in the slushy snow, I didn't have the energy for even a short walk in the evening. I had a gained a bit of weight as well, which bothered my knees when I did attempt to run.

Nate was rarely home in the evening, and I was a little too shy to strike up conversations with strangers at the market or coffee shop. I thought about going to the pub alone, but figured I was more likely to meet men looking for relationships than women looking for friends. By the third week of January, I was desperate for any form of companionship.

Work was my best chance of cultivating a new friendship. Most of the other women were nice, but kept to themselves. Conversations were always cut short the moment Gina was within sight. I finally took the initiative with Louise, whom I had quickly pegged as the most outgoing in the group. She was just as new as I was, and pretty chatty.

"Do you have any plans after work?" I asked her a few minutes before quitting time one Friday.

"I'm working first thing tomorrow morning, so I wasn't planning on doing too much tonight. Why? What's up?"

"I'm off tomorrow and was hoping to do something fun tonight. Do you have the time to grab a drink somewhere before you head home?" I replied with pleading eyes.

"Yeah, we could do that. I've got an hour or so before I really need to be home. I know the perfect bar, and it's close by."

Louise and I walked to a restaurant just around the corner from the store. She had been there before and recommended it due to its mostly male waitstaff and extensive draft beer selection.

I was a little nervous, since technically I wasn't legally allowed to buy alcohol in New York. Fortunately for me, bartenders rarely asked for my ID. I was able to drink in Canada prior to turning nineteen (the Canadian legal drinking age), and although Nate usually bought our beer, no one ever questioned my age when I ordered a drink at a restaurant. If you act confident and comfortable, people assume you must be legal. I was almost of age anyway.

"The guys at Jack Spat's Grill are so pretty that they can't possibly be straight. I might not have a chance of going home with one, but watching them work gives me a focal point for future fantasy," she explained on our walk there.

Louise had a wicked sense of humor, so I was more than happy to let her dominate the conversation. She was born in New Jersey, still lived with her parents, and was just as excited as I was to be working at Century 21. She was saving up for her first apartment.

We ended up staying over two hours and it wasn't until her mother called, asking if she'd be home soon, that we realized how quickly the time had flown by. Louise's mom had dinner on the table, and I needed to get home to make something for Nate and me. We both eagerly agreed to get together again before hugging goodbye.

It felt great to have a friend again. I wasn't currently on speaking terms with either of my sisters, and I had no strong desire to stay in touch with Kassie after I moved out. Besides wishing her a Happy New Year at midnight, I hadn't called Rachel since I moved in with Nate. I'd missed one of her calls while I was at work, and she sent me a message on Facebook asking how things were going in New York. I weakly responded with, *Great, miss you. I'll call soon.*

I was dreading a conversation with one of my favorite people in the world. I didn't want to tell her about the final fight with my parents, or that Nate was never around. I was incapable of lying to Rachel, so I chose to avoid her instead.

I had a slight buzz due to the three pints of beer I drank upon Louise's suggestions. Even though I told her that I preferred wine, she insisted that I try several different specialty craft beers, and I have a hard time saying no. I enjoyed the taste more than the cheap beer Nate bought, but wished I would have ordered the wine I originally wanted. My stomach was bloated and agitated.

I still beat Nate home from work, even though it was after eight o'clock. My belly was too full of beer to crave dinner and there were enough easy options in the fridge for Nate to eat whenever he arrived. Instead of my usual cooking and cleaning, I changed into an oversized shirt that I usually sleep in and curled up on the couch with our comforter wrapped around me. My happy buzz turned into soothing snores in seconds.

"Hey honey, I'm home!" Nate announced himself loudly just before ten o'clock. My eyes blinked rapidly to adjust to the light; then I could see him walking toward me. He crouched next to the couch, kissed my forehead, and asked, "Are you tired? I was hoping we could go out for a drink and celebrate."

"Hi," I whispered as I wiped the sleep from my eyes.

"Can I convince you to go out for a drink?" he asked again, lifting the blanket to rub my bare thigh.

"What time is it?"

"It's still early. Get up! You don't work tomorrow." Nate responded while shaking me playfully. His hands felt cool on my warm body.

I didn't want to disappoint him, but I was no shape to go anywhere. My stomach was churning with beer and there was a dull throbbing resonating from my temples. I pouted and shook my head.

"Come on. Why not?" He was unusually persistent.

"I had a few beers with a girl from work and they were a lot stronger than I thought they would be. I'm not really feeling that great right now." My droopy face confirmed my sincere disappointment.

"Who'd you go with? When?"

"With Louise, right after work. We went to a pub by the store, and she introduced me to some crazy craft beers. She warned me they were strong." I rubbed my face in both hands. "And she was right."

"I guess that's a tough lesson. Do you care if I go without you?" Nate asked, looking adorably innocent.

"I'd prefer you stayed with me, but I won't stop you," I responded honestly.

"Hey, you had your fun. Don't make me feel guilty because I want to go out."

"Sorry, that's not what I meant to do." Feeling like a hungover bitch, I decided to change my tune, "Go, have fun. I'm just going to sleep. We can do something tomorrow night."

"Thanks! You're the best," Nate replied, then kissed me quickly on the forehead. "Get some sleep and we'll spend time together tomorrow."

"Love you," was my simple reply, which was immediately followed by the same from him before he darted into the washroom. I closed my eyes to relieve the pounding and listened for him to flush the toilet and then moments later, shut the main door to our apartment. I fell back asleep within seconds.

At some point throughout the night, I remember staggering from the couch to the bed. I woke up with a dull headache shortly after 6:00 a.m. Nate was not next to me. I assumed he must have crashed on the couch so he wouldn't disturb me, so I took my time getting out of bed. Initially, it didn't even alarm me when I didn't spot a lump on the sofa as I made my way to the washroom. The urgency of my need to pee superseded any concern I had over his whereabouts.

It wasn't until a few minutes later, when I explored our tiny space in a matter of seconds and discovered that he wasn't there, that anxiety set in. Although he kept odd hours, he was usually home shortly after midnight. He always warned me when he'd be exceptionally late. There were no early morning model shoots, at least not that I was aware of.

My heartbeat picked up the pace as I searched the apartment for my phone. I was hoping he'd sent a text, but the last one I had received was sent before he popped back home after work. All it said was: *Put a dress on, we're going dancing.*

I felt awful for turning down his offer to go last night. We barely spent any quality time together, and I passed on the perfect opportunity because I drank more than I should with a woman I barely knew. The kicking myself started almost immediately, and left me with enough guilt that I never made plans to go to the bar with Louise again. We would go for the occasional lunch together instead, but drinking beer together was officially off limits.

I fired off a text to Nate just asking where he was with the hope that my sudden panic and regret would be squashed as quickly as it rose. I stared at the phone, visualizing it would either say he was picking us up fresh baked goods, or he was only a few minutes away from being home to explain. Seconds turned into minutes, and eventually minutes had formed an hour. No response.

I passed time pacing the small walkway between the kitchen and the bedroom. Every time I walked into the kitchen, I'd pinch at something in the fridge to distract me. Inside the bedroom, I'd choke back tears before venturing into the kitchen to stuff them down with a slice of bread or piece of processed cheese.

My mind alternated between imagining he was hit by a car and thinking he could have been beaten up, mugged, and tossed in an alley...or possibly the worst-case scenario, that he'd hooked up with a slut who was willing to dance with him last night, and ended up offering him so much more. I was consumed with a violent combination of fear and insecurities.

Those feelings grew and festered. By eight o'clock, I decided that I would call the police if he didn't at least answer me by ten. He should know by then that I'm awake and worried. I racked my brain to recall if he'd mentioned anything about an early Saturday morning gig, but felt certain he hadn't. It was rare for him to work before noon, especially on a weekend.

I started rationalizing the various scenarios, starting with him being hit by a car. If that happened, he'd still have his phone with him. If he was unconscious, the police or emergency staff would have the phone, so they could notify a loved one—namely me. If he was hurt, someone would have replied to the message.

If he was robbed of his phone and left badly injured or dead in an alley, it could be forever before he was found. The thought of it made me cry uncontrollably. I had to sit on the bed because I was shaking so badly that I couldn't stand any longer. I didn't even entertain the thought of him cheating on me any further. I was already sobbing as if he was dead.

That's the sight Nate walked in on around 8:30 a.m. I was curled up in a ball, crying, wearing only my long night shirt. I was so relieved to hear his voice that I sprang from the bed, leapt into his arms, and wrapped my legs around him. He looked confused by my reaction.

"I'm happy to see you too, my sweetheart." Nate gently separated my head from his shoulder, so he could plant a big kiss on my cheek. "You seem extra happy to see me. Everything okay?"

"Sorry, I was worried. I didn't know where you were, and you hadn't answered my message," I mumbled between sobs.

"I had a few too many drinks, so I crashed on this guy's couch who lives by the bar. My phone died, or I would have sent you a message. Don't cry, my love." He wiped the teardrops from my cheeks.

"I sent you one and didn't hear back. I thought you had been mugged or killed."

"Baby, no one is going to get the better of me. Don't you worry about that." He kissed me again, then lowered me to the floor with his arms still securely wrapped around my waist. I clung to his body a little longer, before regaining my composure and letting go of my unfounded fears.

I was so happy he was home that I didn't question anything else about his night. We were two independently busy people, living in the same place, loving each other whenever we got the chance. At that time, I viewed it as a very mature arrangement.

The following weekend, Nate planned a special dinner and dancing night to celebrate my twenty-first birthday. He told the waiter it was my birthday, which was rewarded with a fancy coffee that had a shot of Bailey's, whipped cream, and a Maraschino cherry on top. After a storybook evening, we made wild, passionate love and fell deep asleep snuggled up against each other.

Although most days were spent apart, Nate always made up for it on our date nights. I was bursting with love for him, yet there was still this heavy pain over not being able to share those feelings with the other people I loved. My relationships with my family and Rachel were struggling to survive the tension over my bold decision and the physical distance that divided us.

Truthfully, they were making more of an effort than me. I sent the occasional brief text, but I hadn't picked up the phone to call my family since Christmas. When my mom left a voice message a few weeks after our fight, apologizing for how we left things, all I did was send a text that said: *All good!* That was how I swept the ugliness under the rug until the beginning of April.

Easter was quickly approaching, and my parents were hoping I'd be coming home for another visit. Both of them called to enquire about my plans. However, I intentionally let it go to voicemail. I was avoiding the dreaded conversation about my new priorities.

Since I was a newer employee, I couldn't get the time off work on a holiday weekend. My parents were willing to pay for my airfare again and work around my schedule, but I couldn't come up with three consecutive days off. The trip was too expensive to make for a less than forty-eight-hour visit.

On the Monday before Holy Thursday, I called the house early in the morning (certain they would all be at work) and left a message saying that I wasn't able to visit. I ended the voicemail with a cheerfully, optimistic "I'll make time to see everyone soon. I promise. Love you!"

I loved my family, but on some level, I knew that I was lying. Nate hadn't expressed any interest in going back home, and I didn't want to go without him. My plan was to first prove that he was worth the sacrifices I'd made, then convince him to show my parents that we were living our best life. I figured once his face was on billboards, they couldn't deny that New York was the right move.

"Does your agent keep a portfolio with all of your work?" I asked Nate one evening in April over dinner.

"They keep the best shots and videos on file," Nate calmly responded.

"What agent are you working with now?" Nate had a tendency to hop between agents. Every gig he mentioned seemed to be booked by a different person.

"Depends on the kind of work. I'll work for whoever books me. Why?" he asked, his eyes piercing. His voice remained perfectly calm, which is why I didn't clue into the bizarre concept of a model working for more than one agent.

"Just curious. Where are your copies?" I persisted, desperately searching for evidence to support his actions.

"What do you mean?" Nate stared at me with a clearly confused look on his face.

"Your copies of the best shots and videos from your paying gigs. I'd like to show my family," I explained.

"Why do you need to show your family my work?" His emotionless voice was tightening with each answer.

I began pacing around the room, intentionally avoiding his suspicious gaze. "I'm proud of you, and I know they would be too if they saw proof of why this move to New York was necessary."

"I don't need your parents to be proud of me. It's just a job, Kate. Plus, why do you care what your parents think? We're building a life together here. This is about us, not them." I was passing in front of Nate as he spoke, and he grabbed onto my waist to hold me in place.

"I know, but I want my family back home to still be a part of our life."

"This is your home now. We're the only family we need. Don't you get that?"

"Of course," I replied, with lackluster enthusiasm.

"We're building an amazing future as high-fashion, affluent New Yorkers." His charming smile broke through the tension. "How wonderful is that?"

I nodded slowly as he stroked my wrist gently.

"Let's make love like wild New Yorkers." His fingertips were gently exploring and tickling my soft ribcage.

Even though my gut was aching with suspicion, I couldn't help but giggle. Nate pulled me in closer and the next thing I knew, I was riding his hard, throbbing cock as he sat on the edge of the couch. My hormones were functioning at a heightened sensitivity. If his hand merely grazed my thigh, it revved my body into action. Sex was the first drug he hooked me on.

In Sheep's Clothing

Ididn't say anything else about his modeling portfolio for several weeks, before my growing curiosity resurfaced. This time, I merely asked if he could at least show the photos to me. He shot me down again, saying booking agencies owned the rights to the files and he couldn't access them. That sounded highly unlikely.

I couldn't shake my concerns, so I offered to go with him the next time he met with his agent. I begged and said that it had nothing to do with my parents, I just wanted to see my love as a model. He told me not to be silly, and that I didn't need to see pictures because I had the real thing in front of me. Of course that led to him grinding against me, and another wild round of ass-grabbing and nipple-biting sex.

The way he dodged my question and turned it into another sexual escapade didn't sit well with me. Nate had been working as a model for over six months, and I had yet to meet anyone from his work. He always had a reason why I couldn't go with him to a gig, and he never brought home copies of the ads he was in. The lack of evidence was causing my gut to ache. I didn't dare accuse him of lying, so I focused on finding clever ways for him to prove himself instead.

"How often do you work with female models?" I asked innocently one Friday night while we were enjoying dinner together after he got back from an afternoon photo shoot.

Nate made a fleeting comment when he first walked in the door that he'd only be home for a couple hours, without offering any exact details. He worked most weekends in the evening, walking the catwalk for niche designers in Soho or Midtown Manhattan. Their events usually ran after the boutiques closed for the night, and he wouldn't get home until hours after midnight. His schedule extended itself later into the predawn hours more and more each week. The extra time could easily be explained by a tryst with a supermodel co-worker.

"Don't start acting jealous, Kate," Nate sternly snapped in my direction. Although the fear of him cheating was a part of my motive, I knew better than to show it. This time my line of questioning had a strategic plan to get some real answers without appearing insecure.

"I'm not jealous. I was actually interested in being one of those women," I confidently beamed back.

"You want to model now?" His eyebrows furrowed as if it was a ridiculous idea.

"Why not? It's working out well for you. I'm pretty easy on the eyes and you can introduce me to your connections," I argued.

"Modeling is brutal for women. Do you really want strangers picking apart your body?" he said curtly. Nate put his fork down, pushed out his chair, and got up from the table. He was walking away in an attempt to end the conversation, but I felt extra-pushy that night.

"I have a thick skin, I can handle it," I answered firmly.

"That skin gets thicker every day, Katie-Bear." I tilted my head like a confused dog, not exactly sure what his words were implying. Nate continued, "I don't care about it and still crave your body, but you're gaining a lot of weight. You would need to lose twenty pounds before they'd even look at you."

Nate words stung deeply. They pierced my skin and caused me to push my half-full plate of dinner away. My new schedule didn't include my usual running or working out, plus my eating habits were no longer as conscientious. My clothes were feeling snug, but I couldn't have gained twenty pounds. Just the thought of it caused a flood of tears to well in my eyes. I tried to choke them back, but out they flowed. Nate noticed immediately.

"See, you think you can handle the criticism, but you're crying right now because I gave you an honest observation. Trust me; you don't want to become a model. I think you're a supermodel anyway, and isn't that what really matters?" Nate tried to reassure me while hugging me from behind, as tightly as he could with the chair wedged between us.

He held me for awhile in silence before gently changing the subject. "Plus, you and I can't model together. I don't want guys looking at you, and I know you don't want to see models watching me strut my stuff." He pulled away and did an overly exaggerated catwalk with kissy-fish lips through the narrow halls of our apartment. I cracked a tiny smile at his silly attempt to make me laugh.

"Just a smile? I'd spend the entire night trying to make you laugh, but I do need to leave for work in an hour. How about I make you a yummy cocktail and we cuddle on the couch watching one of your crappy shows until it's time for me to go?"

I nodded sheepishly. I wasn't interested in the drink, but I had this clingy urge to hold him close to me. While Nate went to the kitchen, I went to the bedroom to change into comfy clothes. We met back in the living room a few minutes later, found a rerun of the Big Bang Theory on TV, and snuggled into one another.

I was trying to enjoy the moment, but I couldn't stop thinking about him being surrounded by models all day. Seeing my new, rounder stomach peeking out over the waist of my yoga pants was not helping matters. I knew I wasn't even close to being overweight, but I was definitely not as fit as when I'd first moved in with Nate. Subconsciously, I kept taking a sip of the way-too-sweet cherry whiskey and 7-Up he made me every time I found myself fidgeting on the couch.

He must have made the drink really strong, because I felt drunk before I finished my glass. I remember his hand grabbing my ass, his mouth exploring my neck feverishly, and then him slowly lowering my head to his fully erect penis. I instinctively opened wide, took him in as deep as I could... and then woke up the next day alone.

It's a frightening feeling to wake up and not be able to remember when you went to sleep. I lay in our bed, clearly recalling Nate's throbbing penis bouncing around the tender insides of my cheeks. I remember every detail from the beginning of our night together. I don't know if I blew him until he exploded in appreciation or if it escalated into one of our usual love-making sessions. I couldn't remember if we said good-bye, or how I ended up in bed completely naked.

I wasn't worried if Nate and I had crazy passionate sex in spite of my obvious intoxication. In fact, that's what I was hoping happened. I was scared that I fell asleep while I was pleasuring him and I ended up sending him to work with blue balls.

My head felt groggy and my stomach was doing flips. I finally rolled out of bed and stumbled to the bathroom. I tasted vomit in my mouth, as if I had been sick, and it initiated a gagging fit. I tried to bring up whatever was troubling my stomach, but I could only spew out toxic water.

After the wretched sounds I was making over and over again, I assumed Nate couldn't possibly be anywhere in the apartment. I was eager to check my phone to see if he sent a message, but the overwhelming urge to shower and wash away the night before won instead.

I felt physically better after my morning routine, but my stomach was still in knots over how things ended with Nate. I killed some nervous energy tidying up our place and ensuring everything, including myself, looked the best it could for whenever he arrived home.

This time Nate didn't show up until mid-afternoon. He brought with him two large submarine sandwiches from the deli around the corner and a tray of coffees from Starbucks. He had a huge grin on his face, inspiring me to do the same. I never did tell him that I couldn't remember exactly how our evening ended, and for a reason unknown to me at the time, it wasn't my last blackout.

Several more weeks went by of simply working and hanging out together in our quaint little apartment. Nothing outstanding happened, although I was still avoiding my family and Rachel, and I was quite certain both had gotten the hint.

When I called my mom on Mother's Day, I rushed the conversation and was off the phone in less than five minutes. The entire month of June passed by without so much as a text between us. I completely fucking forgot Father's Day and felt like an ass, but didn't have the guts to call and apologize.

The few times I spoke on the phone with my parents felt like interrogations, because they questioned everything Nate and I were doing. I made up an excuse to immediately end the call anytime my mother asked for details about the department store or our apartment. I wanted to ensure there would never be any surprise visits. Every word felt like either disapproval or a guilt trip, and they had no idea how shitty our situation was quickly becoming. It was easier to ignore my family completely than face the fact that my rash decision was potentially a failure.

I had to turn things around, so my life choices would be validated. I love summer, so once the weather began to warm up, I constantly tried to convince Nate to do more stuff outside together. We were usually tired from being on our feet all day, but still made a commitment to walk to a local restaurant every Monday night. That was the one day neither of us had to work.

There was an undeniable energy during the summertime in New York. I made a conscious decision to savor as much of it as I could, even without Nate. Although I had planned on spending more of my free time exploring the surroundings around my new hometown, my plans never seemed to work out.

I can recall one early July evening when Nate was going to be leaving for an afternoon photo shoot, and I was planning on using that time to check out several boutiques scattered throughout Manhattan. I asked him if I could go with him into the city, and then we could meet up afterwards for a fancy dinner. He agreed enthusiastically.

A few hours before we were supposed to leave, I felt dizzy and nauseous. Nate told me to lie down and rest for an hour, and that he'd wake me up with enough time for me to freshen up. I woke up alone. Apparently he'd tried to wake me up, but I wouldn't budge.

"You were snoring like you needed the sleep, so I let you be," Nate explained when he got home shortly after midnight. "You can come with me the next time."

He brought home two massive slices of pizza dripping with cheese that we ate in silence before making love and falling asleep together. I should have been able to put the pieces together a whole lot sooner, because similar incidents happened over and over again.

I was getting farther and farther away from the person I wanted to be, and it was destroying my confidence. I didn't have the guts to approach ball-busting Gina with my ideas for the store, and my shifts were spent mainly straightening up clothing racks and costume jewelry.

I had possibly gained somewhere close to twenty pounds (we didn't own a scale), barely spoke to my friends or family, and had this growing doubt that my relationship with Nate was not as great as I thought. I didn't feel overly certain he was being faithful either, and I still had no proof that he was even modeling. Nate had a knack for saying the right thing to ease my worries, but the worry never fully went away.

When my family's annual mid-summer BBQ rolled around the last week of July, I was determined to attend it. I desperately needed a break from New York life, as well as some quality time with my family and Rachel. I made arrangements with my boss to work Friday night and then not come back in until Wednesday morning. I had saved enough for the flight (since I hardly spent my money on going out) that I didn't need to ask my parents for any help with the expense.

I made the bold decision to tell Nate I was going without actually offering an invitation for him to join me. I needed a break from him as well. I waited until after I had bought my ticket and informed my mom about my plans.

I assumed Nate had no interest in going home, plus I didn't need his permission to see my family. We were a modern, independent couple: a point he stressed often. That would be my argument if he had an issue with my decision.

"I bought a ticket to see my family for two weeks from tomorrow. It's a big family gathering, and I haven't seen them in way too long," I casually announced over dinner.

"When are you going?" Nate asked, appearing unrattled by the news.

"I'm leaving here Saturday afternoon and returning Tuesday afternoon. The barbecue is on Sunday. I'll only be gone for a few days."

"Why didn't you tell me sooner?" he asked, with no inflection in his voice.

"I just bought the ticket. I wasn't keeping it from you," I said with a smile, hoping to put an end to his unnecessary interrogation.

"Were you even going to invite me along?" His tone sounded slightly more serious.

"I didn't think you'd want to go home, so I didn't ask."

"It's a family gathering and we're a couple. Am I not invited to your family's house?" Nate's eyes were burning a hole through me; his mood had shifted from cool and calm to angry and agitated.

"If you want to go, I'll ask my mom about it. Do you have enough for the flight?" I enquired, keeping my emotions in check in a pointless attempt not to further upset him.

"I have shitloads of money, but don't bother asking her. I'm your boyfriend, and should be welcome without needing a special invitation."

Nate rose quickly from the table, knocking the chair over backwards. He grabbed his plate and fork and tossed them haphazardly in the sink, causing the plate to chip as it bounced off the metal edge. I was trying to think of a response that would calm him down, but it was too late. I heard the door to our apartment slam as he took off. This was the first time his temper truly frightened me.

I paced the apartment, swearing to myself—*fuck, fuck, fuck, fuck* kept going through my mind. I was caught in this impossible place between hurting the man I loved dearly, or disappointing my loving parents once again. My mind was racing for a compromise that would appease both sides.

I knew my family wouldn't be thrilled if Nate came home with me, but they always tried to give off an impression of acceptance and hospitality regardless of how they personally felt. However, based on the fit he'd just had, it didn't sound like he'd be willing to go. I decided my best bet was to beg him to come with me; when he turned down the offer, he couldn't get mad at me for going alone.

This was my only hope.

When Nate came back from his three-hour walk to cool off, he seemed to be in a much better mood. He walked in, kissed me on the cheek, and put a bottle of vodka and orange juice on the table before sitting down on the couch as if nothing happened. I was puzzled at the change in attitude, but figured it was a great time to test my theory.

"I do want you to go with me, Nate. I didn't mention it originally, because you haven't expressed any interest in going to home. I had no idea you'd want to spend time with my family. I would have asked if I'd known. I'm sorry." I took the seat next to him on the couch, placed my hand on his thigh and gave him the most sincere-looking pout I could fake.

"Okay, I'll go. Give me your flight details, and I'll see if I can get a ticket on the same one," Nate responded calmly, with zero hesitation.

I was shocked. I didn't flinch in a way he could see, but my heart was racing over the potential disaster this could cause. I pulled the printout of my flight ticket from my purse and gave it to him. Nate got up, tucked the paper in the inside pocket of his leather jacket, and went to the kitchen to make us his new favorite cocktail, a screwdriver. I wasn't as big of a fan of it, since every time I had one, I woke up with a massive headache.

I waited until the following day when Nate wasn't home to call my parents about the extra house guest. I was sadly hungover again, since we'd had several strong drinks before tearing the apartment to pieces during our wild romp of make-up sex. It felt like I was still somewhat drunk when I woke up, so I waited a few hours before calling my mom.

"So, there's a slight change of plans, Mom. I don't want to fight over it, but..."

"What? Don't say you're not coming!" My mom interjected before I finished my sentence.

"No, I'm still coming...but so is Nate." I heard her sigh loudly into the phone as I said his name.

"Where's he going to sleep?"

"With me? My bed is big enough," I wishfully suggested.

"You're not married, and you know that goes against our Catholic beliefs. Plus, I don't know him well enough to have him stay in my house. Why can't he stay with his mom?" she asked bitterly.

"She has a boyfriend and is never home. Plus, we want to be together. I guess we could stay at his place," I replied, knowing full well that she would like that idea even less.

"How about he stays there and you stay here? A couple nights apart is not a bad thing."

"He's my boyfriend! We should be together!" I loudly snapped back. "Are you saying he's not welcome in your home? You liked him when you first met him."

"A few things have changed since then, wouldn't you agree?" Her tone came off as condensing, which only fueled my fire.

"It's not fair to judge him so harshly over rumors." I fought back with the same spite in my voice.

"It makes it difficult for us to trust him." She sighed again, unable to disguise her frustration.

"Is he going to be allowed to stay with us or not? Mom, it's both of us or neither." I assertively held my ground. I felt just as justified in my exasperation.

"Yes, it's fine. He can stay here, in the spare bedroom. You're not married. You can at least go a couple days without sharing a bed." This time it was I who sighed. Thankfully, my mom had given in.

Although I was frustrated with her negative attitudes toward the man I planned on marrying one day (a topic I was too fearful to address with either Nate or my family), at least I didn't have to break the news to Nate that he was a feared murderer whom my parents didn't want in their home. We could, at the very least, pretend to be family for the weekend.

I thought maybe this trip would help squash the suspicions I was starting to have about Nate. The fact that he was willing to visit my family showed he truly cared about our relationship. If he was cheating or lying about modeling, he wouldn't be so eager to face my parents.

Yes, that was what I thought...

I remember the day we were leaving for LaSalle in vivid detail. On Saturday morning, he changed the time he was picking me up; he had planned a big surprise for me. He snuck out of our apartment early in the morning to run some mysterious last-minute errand, and asked me to be ready for the airport at 9:30 a.m. My original flight wasn't until 3:50 p.m.; we didn't need that much time to drive there, find a parking spot, and check in.

Nate showed up at 9:20, even earlier than he'd said, with a coffee for both of us. He winked while advising me that he'd put a half shot of espresso in both of our cups. I could tell it tasted different, but didn't give it enough thought at the time.

I guess you could say that it was around this time that I started recalling less and less of the world around me. There were weeks and weeks of blurred memories with details I'm still trying to piece together. I had no idea that we were en route to Niagara Falls until after he passed the exit for the New York airport.

"Wait, don't we turn there?" I asked from the passenger seat.

"That's the surprise!" Nate exclaimed. He was grinning ear to ear.

"We're going somewhere before our flight?"

"Yep! We are certainly going somewhere." His smile was bursting from his face, which made me beam with anticipation. His happy attitude was contagious.

"Are you going to tell me where, or is that part of the surprise?" I teased.

"Where *is* the surprise? Hmm?" he replied with a seductive wink that gave me a warm tingling sensation between my thighs.

"So, you're not going to tell me?"

"All will be revealed in time, my love," Nate assured me.

We drove for hours in near silence. I was quietly watching highway signs, trying to figure out where we were headed. Unfortunately, the espresso appeared to be having the opposite effect than was intended. In fact, I fell asleep staring out the window. I didn't wake up until we were getting ready to cross into Canada at the Buffalo border.

"Come on, babe. You need to wake up before we get to customs," Nate said loudly, shaking me gently.

"Customs? We're not at the airport?" I felt groggy and confused as I tried to assess our surroundings.

"We're driving to your parents with a special stop on the way. That's the surprise." Nate was flashing me that irresistible smile again.

I looked at the clock and instinctually panicked. "We're never going to make it there by tonight!"

"Don't worry, I cleared it with your parents. I rented us a suite in Niagara Falls. They're not expecting us until tomorrow afternoon," Nate calmly explained.

I nodded in agreement, utterly surprised that Nate would ever call my parents. I was sure they were equally shocked to receive the call. I was beyond thrilled at the idea of a romantic getaway, especially knowing he'd spoken with my parents and it didn't end in a total disaster.

Yes, once again, that was what I *thought*.

I wiped the sleep from my eyes, focused on the bright lights in front of me, and managed to act alert enough during the brief questioning period by the authorities. The customs officer scanned our passports and told us to enjoy our evening at the Falls without even popping the trunk.

We stopped at the first Tim Hortons we saw; Nate ran inside to get us coffees and donuts. My legs were still asleep and felt too heavy to move. While he was inside, I searched my purse for my cell phone. I wanted to at least text my parents that I was in Canada and would see them tomorrow. I unsuccessfully searched every inch of my bag, more frantically by the second.

Unless I'm using it or charging it next to our bed, my phone is always kept in my purse. I remembered checking the time on my phone before we left the apartment. I would have put it in my purse when I was done. I remembered seeing it inside my purse before we left. Nate opening the door broke my train of thought.

"Hopefully this will keep you up for the rest of the drive. We're almost there now, sleepyhead."

"Thanks. Have you seen my phone?" I asked. I grabbed the coffee cups from him and placed them in the cup holders between us.

"Nope. The place I rented is just outside the city, closer to Niagara-at-the-Lake. It's not a suite actually. Not sure why I called it that earlier; it's a cabin."

"A cabin for one night?" I quietly thought out loud.

"It's like a fancy suite in the woods. You're worth the money."

"Sounds beautiful. I could have sworn my phone was in my purse." My hand was still hopelessly wiggling around every corner and pocket in my mid-sized shoulder bag.

"You don't need your phone. Let's disconnect for a while, and just enjoy our time together."

"I guess. I'm sure it's back at the apartment."

"Roll your window down. Smell that air? I love it out here! My uncle has a really nice cottage on a lake that we could have stayed at for free, but it's four more hours north of here. It would be a seven-hour drive back to Windsor."

"We could go there next time," I suggested.

"Sure," Nate quickly replied. "We'll go there together."

I was hoping the coffee would help me snap out of the fog I was falling deeper into once more, but it only amplified my grogginess. I fell back to sleep and didn't wake up until we were parked in front of a small cabin, nestled deep within the woods. I could see parts of other cabins through the trees, but we were still fairly secluded.

My eyes would barely focus, so Nate carried me over his shoulder into the house. My body felt like a sandbag when he dropped me onto the bed. I tried to apologize for being so heavy in his arms, but I couldn't form words. I had a hard time saying much of anything for the remainder of that summer.

We never made it to my parents' house.

Nate had drugged me. That wasn't the first time, although I can't be exactly sure when it began. It wasn't until about a week into our new lives in the forest that I found out he had been dealing drugs the entire time we were together.

Nate wasn't a budding supermodel. He was supplying the models with pills. I was slowly piecing together parts of the story; the truth came out one day when Nate was drunk and screaming in a fit of rage.

He propped me up in a wooden chair on the porch so we could have a few drinks outside. I felt like a zombie on the outside, but my mind was able to process most of the moments we shared at the cabin with surreal clarity. I didn't want to engage him, so I pretended my mind shared the same infliction as my numb body. I stared straight ahead in silence as he rambled about how I was responsible for our current predicament.

"This is *your* fault, you know? We could have stayed in happy New York forever, but you kept asking questions. You fucking thought I was a model! I hate models and men who need to prance, parading themselves around for phony praise." Nate loomed over me, spit from his words misting my forehead.

"I wanted to die laughing when you thought *you* could be a model! You're hot, but not model material. Look how quickly you let yourself go. Look how fat you got." He continued berating me as he paced back and forth in front of me.

He lit a fat joint, took two deep hits, and passed it to me. I took a tiny puff and passed it back. Lifting my arm drained every bit of energy I could manage to scrape together. We didn't smoke pot together in New York, but it was becoming a regular habit at the secluded cabin. Then again, nothing we were doing now mimicked the life we'd had only a few weeks prior. Nate was different in the woods.

"I was making huge money. I could make a grand in one night just by making a few deliveries. You ruined that for us. We could have been rich if *you* hadn't ruined everything. Stupid jealous bitch!" He turned back in my direction, and this time he intentionally spat at me with disgust.

I desperately wanted to spit back, but my mouth was too dry and cracked. He rarely gave me anything nutritious or hydrating to drink, and left me tied up when he drove into town, presumably so I couldn't make myself anything.

"I know why you wanted to see your family. I know you were trying to escape. You were going to ruin our life together. We are stuck here because of you," he seethed.

"Now I can never go back to New York. I took every cent Joe had in the safe, plus his stash. I had to make sure we could survive out here, so I robbed a connected man. I took thousands in pills and he will kill me if I ever set foot in the States again. You fucking put a death warrant on my head!" Nate stepped close in front of my chair and put one hand on each wooden arm.

He leaned in and I could feel his warm breath on my forehead. It gave me chills.

"At least you're a great fuck." He reached down, picked me up by the waist, carried me inside, and fucked my lifeless body until we both passed out. When I woke up the next day and remembered everything he had confessed, I puked over the side of the bed—which of course he immediately made me clean up.

My parents were right. He had played me for a fool the entire time. Almost two years wasted, living a lie with a psychopath. Discovering the truth made me boil over with anger. I visualized shoving a handful of pills down his throat. Unfortunately, I didn't know where he was keeping the drugs, nor did I have the strength to wrestle him into swallowing the pills.

If I was going to kill him, I needed to regain my mental and physical capacity. I tried to stop taking the pills after hearing the truth by refusing to eat or drink anything he brought me. My belly rumbled with genuine hunger pangs, and I broke out in cold sweats and had the shakes in less than a day. In a frightening moment during the third day, when I felt like I was dying, he made me beg him for the pills that he was no longer trying to hide. He enjoyed watching me suffer.

"I'll let you eat this yummy chicken wrap and all you need to do is take one pill. How easy is that?" Nate said in the same sweet tone that a parent would use to get their kids to finish their vegetables.

I was sitting at the kitchen table, and he was hovering over me, dangling a tortilla stuffed with sliced deep-fried chicken, mayo, lettuce, and shredded cheese. I don't actually like mayo, but he hadn't let me eat anything for two days. I wanted to rip it from his hand and devour it, but instead I adamantly shook my head no.

"Keep starving yourself. You were getting too fat anyway," he sneered as I shook my head, my lips pressed tightly together. He spitefully tossed the chicken wrap in the garbage.

"Katie-Pie, guess what else I threw in the garbage?" he asked, smug as could be. I tried to burn a hole in his head with my angry stare, but my lack of magical powers made it impossible. I could give him evil looks all day, and it didn't seem to bother him one bit. He didn't care how I felt.

"Your ID, debit card, credit card, and passport are all in a trash bin, far, far away." Nate smiled. "You can stop taking the pills, but it won't do you any good. You're never leaving here."

He grabbed my arm aggressively and dragged me back to the bedroom, then used a scarf to tie me to the bed. He left me there for several hours; my lips were cracked from dehydration, I was shaking from withdrawal, and my stomach was gnawing away on my insides. The utter hopelessness made me crack the next time he came in the room.

"Are you ready to take your pill now, Kate? I'll make you toast if you do. You ruined the yummy chicken wrap, but you can have toast, maybe even with a little butter, if you take your medicine."

I nodded slowly in agreement. I needed something in my belly. I couldn't bear it any longer.

"If you want the toast, I need to hear you ask for your pills." His cruelty was escalating.

"Please," I whispered.

"That's a good girl." He handed me a glass of water and a pale pink pill. He watched as I swallowed it, and asked me to open my mouth afterwards to prove it was gone. He then made me two pieces of buttered toast, which he wouldn't hand off until I thanked him for making it.

I'm now grateful for those pills and the marijuana, because they cast a deep fog over most of what I experienced in the woods. Our new routine consisted of getting fucked up, violent sex, and too much sleep.

My next clear memory wasn't until several weeks later, the night of the fire.

Up in Flames

Nate had removed all clocks and calendars (if there were any to begin with), but I estimated we had been at the cabin for more than a month. Summer was transitioning into autumn, and the leaves were just beginning to fall from the trees. Although it wasn't cold out, the aggressive humidity had subsided.

Nate wanted a fire outside. He cleared the area surrounding the built-in metal pit and pulled a bag of dry wood out of his trunk. Holding my hand, he carefully led me toward one of two wooden chairs he positioned around the firepit.

I wasn't as lifeless as I had been the first weeks we were at the cabin, since I was intentionally trying to wean myself off of whatever drugs he was feeding me. Now that he wasn't hiding it in my food, I had some control over how much I took. I would take it from him as if I desperately needed it and then tuck it between my gums and my cheek, at the back of my mouth. I would spit it out once I had the chance. I was still absorbing enough to fight off the withdrawal, but I didn't feel like a lifeless zombie.

I had a clever hiding spot for the pills I didn't finish. My plan was to sneak enough into his food to knock him unconscious, so I could escape while he was out. By the night of the fire I already had eleven partial pills saved, hidden inside a rolled-up pair of socks. I thought it would be enough to immobilize him, but I was still too weak and scared to run from him.

It felt like I was in the middle of a bad dream, yet I was so petrified by the thought of what would happen once I woke up from it that I wasn't ready to face reality. The thought of breaking free paralyzed me more than the drugs.

I sat quietly, lost in my thoughts, while Nate built an excessively large fire in front of us. The air was cold for late summer weather, due to recent rain showers. Although we were both wearing enough clothing that we didn't need the additional warmth, Nate insisted I wear the wool gloves and hat that he'd picked up for me a few weeks before. Brief moments like that would remind me of the man I fell in love with, but it never lasted long. He'd open his mouth and I'd be flung back into the nightmare.

"How long do you think we can hide out here?" He turned away from the fierce flames and questioned me with his hands firmly on his hips.

I shrugged with a sincerely confused look on my face.

"This fucking *sucks!*" he suddenly shouted into the slowly darkening evening sky.

I nodded in agreement, praying he was feeling guilty and considering setting me free.

"We can't go back," he mumbled to himself, continuing to stare me down. "You could destroy me."

"I wouldn't," I looked him directly in the eyes for the first time since I'd discovered the horrifying truth of our relationship.

"Why wouldn't you? Look what I've done to you. I can't let you go free; you'll put me in jail. You would destroy me." He moved a step forward, bridging the small gap between us.

"I wouldn't. I promise you, I won't say *anything*," I said. I tried to speak a little louder, with slightly more forced conviction.

"Yeah, you would. I saw you hiding pills in that pair of socks. Were you going to drug me? You're promising me that you won't rat me out, but you're currently trying to kill me?" His voice balanced smug self-confidence and devilish desires.

My lips made the "No, no, no," sounds, but my mind was screaming *fuck, fuck, fuck.* My plan was ruined; Nate knew all about it. I could feel the vomit rising from my stomach and my hands trembled under his deadly glare.

"Liar," he stated matter-of-factly. "I know better than to trust you. Don't worry, I have a simple way to fix this problem."

He stared up at the sky as if he was looking for divine guidance. His sudden silence amplified the chirping of nearby insects. I was furtively working up enough energy and fortitude to thrust my body into Nate, hoping I could knock him into the fire blazing behind him. I had a bad feeling about his intentions and felt compelled to act first.

Just as I was mustering the courage to push him away from me, Nate shouted at me. He was bending so far forward that he was mere inches away from my face. "Once again, it's up to me to fix everything!"

Nate leaned in even closer; his lips were tickling mine. Terrified goosebumps covered my skin. The urge to kick him in the balls hard enough to send him backward into the flames crossed my mind, but not soon enough. His violent instincts were more fine-tuned than my own.

Nate reached out and grabbed a wad of my hair on the top of my head. He squeezed his fist tightly, ripping several strands from my scalp. He then used the tangled mess to yank me into a standing position. His other hand had a firm grip on my hip, pain from the jerking motion radiating down my spine.

"You will burn for your sins."

That's the last thing I heard Nate say that day. He tossed me like a ragdoll into the massive fire. My tacky blend of wool and polyester clothing instantly burst into flames. I remember the overwhelming heat and a bone-chilling sensation that my flesh was melting from my body. I heaved myself out of the fire as quickly as he'd tossed me into it, but it was too late. I was a ball of flames hurtling into a forest of trees.

I didn't want to go deeper into the forest, so I dove to the damp, cold ground. My bones bounced off the hard terrain as I rolled around the rugged soil, screeching at the top of my lungs. I felt every ounce of water drain from my body. My lips crackled with the heat. Small puddles scattered throughout the forest floor caused my skin to sizzle. I didn't feel pain necessarily, because my body had gone into shock.

My screams stemmed from being awoken from a horrible dream and realizing reality was far worse than I could imagine. Somehow, someway, I rolled around enough to put out the fire that was hungrily consuming my skin. I continued to howl into the sky, praying someone would hear me, before at some point finally passing out due to shock.

When the world went black in the forest and I could feel my skin melting from my body, I assumed that this would be the end of my story. I gave in to the numbness, feeling like I had failed the life I was given. I didn't feel any more fight left in me to go on. Thankfully, my survival wasn't left totally in my own hands.

By the grace of God, I was found and rushed to a nearby hospital within the hour. Someone had in fact heard my screams, saw the fire, and witnessed Nate's car leaving the sleepy backwoods area at warp speed. When the local hunter saw my burned, smoking body on the ground, he immediately called the police.

I have very little recollection of my first few days in the hospital, except that I was uncontrollably shaking and sweating, or vomiting and drooling, due to a combination of opioid withdrawals and my lack of skin.

The police weren't able to identify me until I regained consciousness. They didn't have a photo of my face before the fire, and the bandages were covering too much to take a recognizable image. The local news only reported that a young woman had been burned in a fire, and the suspect was still on the loose. My story didn't receive any national coverage.

I refused to give them my family's contact information once I awoke. I was ashamed of choosing an asshole over the family that had always been there for me, and embarrassed by what I imagined I looked like underneath the bandages covering two thirds of my face. I didn't actually know how bad it was at that time, since the hospital staff had wisely removed every mirror from my room.

The police interviewed me twice while I was in the hospital. I eagerly offered every detail I could about how Nathan looked, the things he'd said, and what had happened during those last few months of our relationship. During that vulnerable moment in time, I had the courage to admit everything instead of wallowing in shame.

Sadly, it didn't seem to matter. My temporary strength soon faded. Nathan was still on the loose; I wasn't coherent enough to be interviewed until my third day in the hospital, so he had a significant head start. The thought of him being free when I would be trapped in this hideous skin for the rest of my life turned my courage into anger and bitterness.

I wasn't interested in recovering or returning to normal life. I had no idea what that life could possibly entail now that I was a college dropout who couldn't go home. Who would hire someone with a melted face? Self-pity consumed me.

It was the hospital that recommended I go to a women's shelter after I insisted that contacting my family was not an option. I feared returning home for more reasons than just the shame of admitting such a horrible mistake or the gruesome scars covering my face, torso, hands, and feet: I knew it would be easier for Nathan to find me at my parents' house. I feared transferring the horror he'd put me through to those I loved.

Once my vitals were steady and my feet were healed enough that I could walk on my own, the hospital had no choice but to discharge me. A nice nurse named Nancy called Doris at a shelter in a nearby town and made arrangements for her to pick me up.

I was shocked that two total strangers were willing to care for me when I didn't have the guts to call my parents, who deep down I knew would do the same. It was my fault I was in this mess, my fault for not listening to them, and my guilt would not allow me to become a further burden to my family.

I adored Doris the moment I met her. She reminded me of my grandma. While Nancy explained, she took detailed notes on how to change my bandages and apply the antibiotic ointment. With my permission, we made the decision to leave Doris in charge of the bottle of painkillers. I had no desire to become a zombie again and was confident I had kicked the mental aspect of the addiction during the nine days I spent at the hospital. However, you can never be too safe.

I barely took any pain medication, anyway When the pain was bad, I would just close my eyes and imagine that I could transfer the agony to

Nathan. I would envision flames engulfing his body, and his face contorting as he howled in pain. I desperately wanted Nathan to burn for *his* sins.

I started referring to him as Nathan again after the fire, because the name Nate filled me with an uncontrollable rage. I also insisted on being called Katelyn, and would immediately correct anyone who tried to shorten it to Kate. I was daydreaming about his arrogant face bursting into flames when Doris interrupted my destructive train of thought.

"Nancy gave me your pain medication and your clothes the police gathered from the cabin. We'll go through it back at the house, wash anything that needs it, and figure out what else you might need." Doris held up a standard reusable shopping bag, showing off the pathetic contents of my life.

I stared at the floor as tears formed in my eyes. I didn't want a stranger to see me cry. Everything I owned had been reduced to one small, cheap, canvas bag. Although I felt utterly worthless and hopeless, I gathered enough strength to shake it off, stand up, and slowly follow her outside.

When we got to the shelter, Doris introduced me to several other women, but my mind didn't absorb any of their names the first few days. I was still trying to process how I went from a promising university student to a disfigured refugee hiding out in a home for abused women.

I told Doris I had a headache and needed to lie down. I lay in bed for a while, straining to listen to muffled conversations outside the bedroom door. I imagined they were trying to guess why half of my body was covered in bandages—unless Doris had already filled them in.

Eventually I must have fallen asleep, because the next thing I remember was a young woman standing over me. Her dark, tightly-wound curls seemed to bounce up and down as she spoke. "Sorry to wake you, Katelyn. We're about to eat dinner if you're hungry."

It felt like a lifetime had passed since I ate, so I nodded slowly. The right side of my neck was covered in thick gauze and surgical tape, restricting my movement.

"Do you need any help standing?" Her big dark eyes were fixated on my heavily wrapped feet.

"No, I can stand up." Although my feet were covered in thick bandages like socks, the pain had subsided significantly. The skin was no longer raw, and the bandages were only there to prevent infections in the newly forming skin.

"Okay, I'll tell Doris you're coming." The tiny angel (who I later learned was named Maya) responded with an overly enthusiastic smile.

I'd slept in the same yoga pants and tank top I had worn in the hospital. The canvas bag Doris carried for me was on top of an old dresser next to the bed. I found a pair of hospital scrub pants that weren't mine (possibly a donation from someone at the hospital) and a soft cotton t-shirt that Nathan had picked up for me while we were staying at the cabin.

Although I knew changing wouldn't be easy, I didn't want to ruin everyone's dinner with my foul-smelling clothing. When I lifted the tank top over my head, I accidentally ripped the tape off my left wrist, exposing fresh pink skin. When I slowly pulled the pants down over my feet, I felt pain radiating through my frail, thin limbs. Putting on clean clothes was just as challenging, but I made it through.

There was a bathroom across the hall from the bedroom I was in. I popped inside so I could pee and freshen up the best I could. I used the toilet first, intentionally avoiding the large mirror I sensed on the right. However, I couldn't avoid it when I went to wash my hands.

I was always the pretty one.

The reflection in the carefully polished unframed glass was hideous. One-third of my forehead was a pale pink that contrasted drastically with the light tan color of the other two-thirds. My neck and right cheek were still heavily bandaged, yet my mind supplied an image of the disfigurement that must be hiding underneath. I imagined it must look similar to the melted candle wax in the shape of an abstract Picasso ear that clung to the side of my head. Thanks to Nathan, I now had one normal ear and one freakishly small, non-functioning blob.

I had no eyelashes on my right eye, and my hair was noticeably shorter. Although I remember the smell of burning hair from that night, I didn't realize my hair was on fire when I was rolling around on the ground. I assumed that was the reason for my new too-shabby-to-be-chic hairstyle.

I was no longer the pretty one.

I never made it to dinner. I crawled back in bed instead. Maya brought me a banana, a blueberry muffin, and a bottle of water when she discovered I wouldn't be joining them. I felt guilty that these complete strangers were caring for me when I was too depressed to care for myself.

Every time I closed my eyes, I kept picturing life as Gollum from *The Lord of the Rings*. I didn't want to live the rest of my life as an ugly ogre, and I had moments when I wished I had died in the fire. Dying was the only escape I could see.

I wasted the next few days at the shelter feeling sorry for myself. I spent most of my time in bed, in total silence; I only got up to the use the washroom, eat the minimal food required to survive, or change my bandages. The other women tried to engage me in conversation, but their words didn't register. The most they got from me was a nod or a half-hearted smile. I felt their pity and was embarrassed by it.

Doris suggested I speak with a therapist named Janice who visited the shelter regularly. I knew how badly I needed to talk to someone about everything that happened, but fought the invitation for several days. I was so ashamed of how horribly I had ruined my life. I wasn't ready to admit it out loud.

The third night, I woke up suddenly in the middle of the night. My skin was drenched in sweat, my body throbbing with pain, and my heart racing at rapid speed. I dreamed that I was running into the woods while on fire, and every step I took ignited the trees surrounding me. I smelled the burning hair and felt the fierce heat throughout my body just as I had a month prior.

Realizing it was a dream, I closed my eyes tightly and envisioned slitting my wrists in the shower with a razor. I thought that would be the only way to end the misery consuming me. Luckily for me, I still needed Doris's help bathing, since portions of my right arm and side were too sensitive to get wet. That sweet woman saved me in more ways than she knows.

Standing with Survivors

On my fifth morning at the shelter, Maya left the door to our room open when she went to prepare breakfast. I could hear the other women talking and laughing as they bustled around the kitchen making a meal together. Every time one of them visited my room to bring food or invite me to watch TV, they were so warm and cheerful.

A light went off inside me as I lay in bed watching the sunrise through the bedroom curtains. All of the women I met must be survivors of some sort, I realized. They wouldn't be staying at a shelter unless it was their only choice. I was so busy feeling sorry for myself that it hadn't occurred to me that the women serving and caring for me had possibly experienced the same or worse abuse as I had gone through with Nathan.

I took a deep breath and announced to the empty room, "It's time you think about someone other than yourself." I stood up, slowly put one foot in front of the other, and made my way into the kitchen. I walked in and cheerfully said, "Good morning!"

"It is a good morning! How are you feeling, Katelyn?" Doris asked with a hopefully smile.

"I feel good. I want to help with breakfast," I announced proudly.

"Sure. You could help Angie set the table," Doris offered.

"Okay. I just want to say thank you first. I'm grateful for everything everyone has done to help me the last few days. I'm done with my pity party." My eyes filled with softly flowing tears as the words trickled from my lips.

"You're very welcome."

"We're here for you."

"We've all had our own pity parties."

"We understand."

One after another, those women started to repair my broken heart. The love and compassion I felt from these kind-hearted warriors awoke my desire to live again. I helped set the table that morning, and then asked Doris afterwards if I could speak with the therapist. I didn't want to continue lying in bed wishing that I was dead.

Prior to meeting Nathan, I was a beautiful, well-rounded, ambitious student with a promising future. The only thing that had permanently changed was my appearance, and even that would improve with time. My hair would grow back, and I was already seeing dark strands peeking through where my eyebrows and lashes used to be. I could use concealer to fix the change of skin tones, which could possibly repair itself over time.

More important than the burns scarring my skin was the fact that I was still alive. I had survived for a reason, and I couldn't let Nathan be the death of me. He doesn't deserve to be free from the consequences of what he did.

I needed to live long enough to watch him get caught and sentenced for the horror and abuse he put me through. My new self-awareness made me realize that he most likely was responsible for Jeannie's death as well. That meant if he walked free, it was highly likely that he would do it again, to some other girl.

I couldn't let that happen. He was a cold-blooded murderer who must be locked up. That was the first thought I shared when I met with Janice, the house's trained counselor, later that afternoon. I told her that I wanted to live just so I could watch Nathan suffer for what he did to me.

"That's a normal and expected feeling. Eventually the anger will subside, but it's good to express it verbally rather than keep it bottled up inside." Her gentle encouragement slowly nurtured the entire story from my soul.

"He convinced me that he was a good guy. That's the man I knew. He was loving and generous. By the time I saw his true colors, it was too late; he'd kidnapped me, and we were living in the woods. I had no idea he would do something like that," I calmly explained.

"Unfortunately, abusive people are skilled at manipulation. That's how they're able to control their victims."

"I feel like such a fool." My voice cracked with each word.

"It wasn't your fault." Janice looked me directly in the eye, saying each word slowly and purposefully.

That wasn't the first time I heard those words; people had said that to me several times since the fire. Both police officers said the same thing after they interviewed me. Nancy, the nurse, had said it as well, when I turned down her suggestion of calling my parents. Those four words were finally feeling real. This was *Nathan's* fault, not mine.

I spent the next few weeks adjusting to my new environment. I asked the other women question after question about how they ended up here, to the extent that I kept apologizing for being so nosey. I guessed that I was the youngest in the house, and I felt I could learn something from the other ladies. Most were willing to share the broad picture of what they went through in a matter-of-fact way that didn't reveal too many details or raw emotions.

About three or four weeks after I arrived, a woman named Pam (actually Sam) spilled her guts one night, slowly inspiring the rest of us to do the same. She was running from the police and lied to protect her identity. Her vulnerability and hearing how quickly her life was suddenly twisted upside down made me feel better about my own mistakes.

Through listening to such a diverse group of survivors, I learned how to condense my experiences into an emotionless statement that didn't cause me to painfully relive every moment. I absorbed several survival lessons that will stick with me for the rest of my life.

It was an older woman named Donna who finally convinced me to reach out to those who loved me. "I have a twenty-one-year-old son named Aiden. When Aiden went off to college, I finally left his father. I can't reach out to him because I don't want my ex to find me. It breaks my heart that I can't talk to my son. I'm sure your parents would give anything to hear your voice right now."

I knew she was right, but I was still worried about their reaction. I was also wondering why they hadn't looked for me. There was no missing person report when the police interviewed me. They should have gone to the police when I didn't come to visit as planned at the end of July. Over two months went by without contact, but no one cared enough to report me missing. It didn't make sense.

I wasn't certain that my parents would be pleased to hear from me, so I tried calling Rachel first. Unfortunately, she didn't answer. I left her a voice message, begging her to call me back. "I know I've been gone too long, and I'm sorry. I want to talk. Please call me."

It took another two hours without hearing back from Rachel before I worked up the courage to call my parents. It was time for me to face the consequences of my decisions. My mom answered in her always profes-sional, manner. "Hello."

"Mom, I'm sorry," was all I could manage before bursting into heavy, choked-up sobs. As the flood gates opened and I couldn't manage another word, I heard my mom whispering back.

"It's okay, dear. It's okay. It's okay, dear." I could hear the tears clog-ging her throat.

It was several minutes before we were able to have real dialogue. I eagerly admitted that I was wrong about Nathan. Without going into any details, I explained that he'd tried to hurt me, and I was staying somewhere safe until he was arrested. My mom let me know that an officer had been to their house looking for Nathan but only left a card, asking them to call if they saw him. She'd assumed it had to do with the Jeannie incident from the prior summer.

"Did he do something else? Can I tell the officer that you called me? Are you in trouble? Where is Nate?" My mom's voice was shaky as she rambled off questions.

"You can tell the police, but they've spoken with me already. I'm not in trouble." I focused on keeping my voice steady to ease her concern.

"What did he do?" she asked hesitantly.

"He tried to hurt me, and succeeded. I'm healing quickly and being cared for by the kindest women."

"I can care for you. What did he do? Where are you?" I could hear the pain in her voice.

"It would be really hard for him to find me here. However, he's been to your house before and I don't want to attract him to your house again. I need to stay where I'm safe until he's caught. I'm sorry, Mom." And before she could respond, I added, "I love all of you."

"We love you too, and will do whatever you need us to do," she conceded compassionately.

"I know. Hopefully they'll catch him soon and I can come home."

"I hope so, too. Please be safe. We miss you."

"I'll call back later this week. Bye, Mom."

"Bye my dear, sweet Katelyn. It was so good to hear your voice."

"Yours too," I whispered before quickly hanging up. My eyes were filled with tears again. I was so grateful that she was so easily forgiving, especially considering what I found out during our next conversation. I needed to hear her voice again and I had a few unanswered questions, so I called her again the next day.

"I wanted to reach out sooner, but I didn't know if you were angry with me. I was surprised that I hadn't been reported missing after I didn't show up in July," I calmly explained.

"Well, you did send us a text saying you weren't coming."

"No, I didn't."

"We got a text saying you had to work. I responded back saying you'd be missed and that we hoped to see you soon."

"I haven't had a phone since we left to go home that weekend."

"So, you didn't send me any of those texts?" she asked.

"There was more than one?" I replied.

"Yes, we had several nasty fights by text, where you accused me of always seeing the worst in people and trying to control you. I kept insisting we talk on the phone, but you wouldn't answer my calls. You told me to stop bothering you sometime in August. That was the last time you answered one of my texts."

"Mom, that wasn't me. It must have been him."

"I thought you were still mad at me." I could hear the snotty tears coating her throat.

"No, Mom. I was wrong about him. I was *very* wrong," I replied, choking back loud sobs of my own.

"Guys can be deceptively charming. I'm just happy you are safe now."

"Me too."

That conversation with my mom inspired a second attempt at reaching Rachel. I realized he could have picked a horrible fight with her as well, and she might be justified in not calling me back. This time, I rambled as much of the story as I could into her voicemail as I could possibly fit in before it timed out.

"Rachel, I'm sorry. If you received mean texts from me, it wasn't me. It was him. He did it to my family, too. He drugged and kidnapped me. I miss you. Please call me. I need to talk to you," I begged into the recording.

This time, she returned my call within five minutes. She hadn't returned my earlier call because Nathan had sent a text from me calling her a nosy bitch when she asked why I hadn't visited my family like I'd planned. She was already frustrated with me for avoiding her, and that text was the final straw.

Luckily for me, Rachel's response to the details I was willing to share was just as supportive and sympathetic as my mom's. However, I didn't mention the fire or the frightening scars that covered my body. I knew she'd worry more about me if I did.

Although I wasn't comfortable breaking the tragic news to my family or best friend via phone, I was finally opening up about it. Janice gently asked the right questions and inquired on how the change in my appearance was affecting my self-esteem. I was still doing my best to avoid looking into a mirror; I couldn't help but think I was a hideous beast.

The more I talked about the fire with Janice, and eventually other women in the house, the less the images of my face haunted me. I stopped wishing Nathan would burst into flames and started searching my memory for facts that could help with the investigation. That's when I remembered his uncle's cottage. They had asked me before if I could think of where he might hideout and that was definitely a possibility.

I passed the tip along to the detective, who then got the address through Nathan's mom. She told the detective that she hadn't mentioned it earlier, since it belonged to her deceased husband's brother. Nathan hadn't been to the cottage in Northern Ontario or to his uncle's home in Michigan since his father's funeral. She didn't realize Nathan remembered his uncle, or that the cottage even existed.

A stakeout was planned within three days of me suggesting it as Nathan's possible hideout. Thankfully, they caught him off guard and he was arrested without incident. Due to him being a suspect in one murder and another attempted murder, they ruled to hold him without bail until the trial. Not even Nathan was sneaky enough to slip through prison bars.

It was November 5th, and the first day I'd felt safe in over three months. I called my parents that afternoon as soon as I got the news of his capture, and they insisted on picking me up at the shelter the very next day.

Doris and Donna quickly planned a good-bye party with cake and ice cream. Although I had only been there a little less than two months, they already felt like family. I wouldn't have survived the experience without their kindness.

As much as I adored Doris, nothing felt as reassuring as the hugs I got when my parents and sister arrived. My mom was first and clung to me for at least ten minutes, sobbing into my shoulder. I could tell that the sight of my burns had caught her off guard. My father gave me a firm, all enveloping hug while gently shaking the tears from his cheeks. Tina, who insisted on coming along for the ride, snuck her way into my hug with dad and didn't let go until long after he did.

They did their best not to stare at my scars, which were nowhere near as noticeable as I had feared they would be. We kept the conversation in the car pretty light, focusing on Tina's athletic triumphs and Amy's sudden engagement to Michael. My dad was quiet and focused on the road. Mom nibbled on her lower lip.

I wasn't sure how it would feel, living with my family after being free for so long. However, it ended up feeling more empowering than it ever was with Nathan. My parents never tried to control me or demean me. They genuinely wanted me to heal, recover, and succeed. We quickly fell back into a healthy routine with one another, and all former follies faded away.

Although they were concerned that it would hurt my emotional progress, my parents supported my decision to testify against Nathan. They knew I needed justice. I waited almost ten months after his capture for the trial. Even though he was behind bars leading up to it, I still felt like my life was on hold. I was planning for my future, but couldn't convince myself to follow through until I knew he was locked up for good.

I looked into the University of Windsor to see what credits I could use toward my Bachelor of Education, once I was ready. My passion for fashion was gone; it had been replaced with a strong desire to teach young women. I was particularly interested in teaching social studies, or possibly at-risk youths at the high school level. My gut was certain that was the path I needed to be on.

I spent a lot of my free time reading, both as an escape and for educational purposes. Studying the laws, especially in regards to domestic violence and drugging women, held my attention. Based on the statistics I read, men drugging and taking advantage of women was more common that I could possibly fathom. I was inspired to use my story to warn other women, and hopefully make experiences like mine less frequent.

Justice Served

Nathan would not get away with what he did to me. Every time I looked in the mirror, my eyes immediately focused on the hideous scars that tainted my once unblemished skin. He tried to take away my life. In the process, he stripped me of my former physical appeal. I wasn't Miss Pretty anymore. I felt like Miss Foolish or Miss Naive, and it was all because of him.

My father insisted on hiring a trial coach to run through my testimony with me, and the prosecutor went over my story in excruciating detail. I eagerly accepted all the help I could get. I pumped myself up and felt confident that we would put Nathan away for a very long time.

He would finally pay for his sins.

Despite being gung-ho throughout the grueling months leading up to it, the first thing I did on the morning of the trial was vomit. My stomach was so turbulent that I couldn't even keep down coffee. My hands were shaking and my heart pounded inside my chest.

Nathan's pretty face crossed my mind, and I was suddenly worried that he'd be able to cast me under his spell again. I was concerned the jury would fall for his good looks and manipulative charm. Every part of me wanted to crawl into my childhood bed and never come out.

Instead of going back to my room where it was safe, I went to visit my father in his den. I could tell he was nervous too, because he was just sitting in his chocolate brown leather chair, staring at a photo of me and my sisters when we were little girls. The resting hand in his lap was vibrating rapidly, side to side. Of course, my father acted like he had everything under control once he noticed that I was in the door frame.

"Good morning, Katelyn. How are you doing?" My dad asked with a calm, reassuring voice.

"How bad would it be if I don't show up today? It's not like he'll be found innocent just because I'm not there. Right? It's not necessary for me to actually get up on that stand, is it?" I asked innocently, trying to hide my nerves as well.

"You know that we will support your decision no matter what...but you *are* the star witness. He could go free without your testimony," my dad responded, holding nothing back as usual.

"I know. I know." I nodded, mentally pumping myself back up to lock that asshole away forever.

My nerves never settled, though. I puked again at the courthouse, but the thought of him going free was enough motivation for me to show up. His arrogant face and the subtle, flirtatious gestures he made toward me as he watched me walk into the room eradicated the little bit of love and sympathy that still tugged at my heart.

In front of those jurors, I referred to what he did to me at the cabin as rape. Since Nathan and I had sex countless times prior to the drug-induced, rough sex at the cabin, I wasn't sure if people would believe that it was actual rape. I was technically still his girlfriend then, and I'd willingly had sex with him many, many times before.

The main difference is that I didn't have a choice at the cabin. When I explained the details of what happened to the police while I was in the hospital, they said there was evidence of rape. When I met with the therapist at the shelter and more recently in Windsor, they pointed out that any sex while I was drugged would be considered rape. I had a hard time accepting that he raped me because I once was so convinced that he loved me.

I had significantly downplayed the events of my last few months with Nathan to my family. I didn't want anyone to know how foolish I had been. Even though I knew the words would break my parents' hearts, I couldn't hold anything back when the prosecutor asked me exactly what happened.

"Nathan drugged me without my knowledge, stole my cellphone, and kidnapped me. He took me to a cabin in the middle of the woods, continued to slip drugs into my food and drink, and repeatedly raped me. When he was finally finished with me, he threw me into a large fire, hoping I'd burn to death." Every word was pronounced with the utmost confidence and clarity. I didn't want the jury to have a single doubt in their mind.

I was asked more questions by both sides and gave the various details I could remember through the toxic haze. His lawyer tried to insinuate that I was an addict who took the drugs by choice. Nathan testified that we went to the cabin together as a way to escape the tyranny of my overbearing parents. He referred to us as a rebellious young couple in love. How convincing he sounded as he lied through his teeth made my skin crawl.

"I would never hurt Kate. I love her. She fell into the fire on her own. She's only blaming me now because she's afraid of disappointing her parents." Cockiness spewed from his mouth without conscience. Luckily, the prosecutor was prepared for his bullshit.

"If she fell into the fire, why did you leave her there to die? Why wouldn't you call for help?" my fierce lawyer fired back with confidence.

Nathan stumbled with his deceitful response. "I didn't...'cause I couldn't. We had a fight earlier that night. I was tired of her abusing drugs and insisted she quit. I left before she fell in the fire."

"You were seen driving away from the cottage right after the fire." The prosecutor repeated the facts of the case that were already established through previous witness testimonies.

"I bet she threw herself in the fire because I was threatening to leave her. She's nuts!" Nathan's convincing charm was beginning to waver.

"A mere moment ago, you testified that she fell into the fire. Now, you're saying it happened after you left. Which is the truth?"

"I don't know; I wasn't there! It's all her fault." Nathan pointed directly at me. I remained calm and let my lawyer finish him off.

"If you haven't done anything wrong, why did the police find you hiding out in your uncle's cabin?"

"I needed a vacation after being with her. Is that a crime?" His voice dripped with contempt.

"No, but drugging, kidnapping, raping, and attempting to kill my client is a series of heinous crimes. It's also criminal to flee the scene of a crime, especially while your victim was *literally* on fire. No further questions."

Despite his best efforts, there was enough evidence and testimony that the jury saw through his lies. I wept tears of relief when they announced the verdict. Nathan was found guilty on all charges, and sentenced to fifteen years in jail with no chance at parole for ten years.

Unfortunately, he was never tried in Jeannie's murder. There wasn't enough evidence to connect him to her beating, despite the overwhelming suspicion. I knew he deserved longer, but was satisfied that I had at least another ten years without worrying that he'd find me.

The freedom I felt when he was finally captured didn't even compare to the day I heard that verdict. My cheeks formed a permanent smile, and I was speechless for hours. Family and friends hugged me, gushing over the outcome, and I could only nod enthusiastically. My family took us all to Red Lobster for dinner to celebrate the victory.

That's when I got my new nickname.

I noticed my dad couldn't stop staring at me from across the table, and assumed he was focusing on the scars along my cheek and neck. I thought *it must bother him that I'm no longer his little Miss Pretty*. It's hard not to be self-conscious over my far-from-flawless appearance, so my instinct was to use my hand to cover the areas with skin discoloration. My dad saw the insecurity in my eyes as I shifted my body in shame.

"Katelyn, you don't have to cover those scars. You're still Miss Pretty, and what's more, you're now also Miss Braveheart. Those marks are a symbol of the courage you showed in the courtroom today. I couldn't be more proud of you," my dad eagerly reassured me.

From that moment forward, my dad always referred to me as the brave one. Although I felt foolish for getting myself into such a horrific situation, I felt fortunate that I'd survived the fire and had the guts to seek justice. Nathan tried to kill me, but I was too tough to go down without a fight.

It had felt like I was living in a perpetual nightmare, where my only goal was to escape further torture. After the trial, I knew my torturer would be locked up for a long time. It meant I could give my attention to recovery and rebuilding without that fear of him gnawing on my neck. I will always have the scars he left on my skin, but my heart has finally healed.

I now have the confidence to share my story of survival with others, in the hope it will serve them well—as both a warning of the worst that can happen, and a reminder that the best futures often follow the most challenging pasts.

As I recalled and retold the events that led to the fire, I saw the signs that something wasn't right were flashing all along. I had ignored my instincts and continuously believe his word over my own feelings. I was so desperate to feel loved that I let him persuade me into anything. Now that the smoke has cleared, I see Nathan for the man he was all along.

Once I was able to let go of the fantasy that I wanted him to be, I found the real me. My ambition, diligence, and confidence returned with time. I enrolled in university again and ended up graduating with honors from the University of Windsor Bachelor of Education program. I found part-time work as a tutor while I waited for a full-time classroom position.

Although it took time, I regained everything Nathan stole from me (my poor right ear being the only exception). I didn't think I could ever trust another man, but I even fell in love with a genuinely sweet gentleman. I stand my ground with him probably more than necessary, but he's very understanding. He knows what I went through, and is incredibly patient.

Nathan tried to burn my world down, but I had the resilience to rebuild it, one brick at a time. Once my confidence rebounded, I felt certain that no one could extinguish my flame again.

Now, I am Miss Braveheart.

Miss Braveheart

By Jenn Sadai

Her fierce beauty was celebrated right from birth.
Long before most, she recognized her worth.
Confidence beamed from her reflection in the mirror.
Fragile as its glass, as looks fade year after year.

Flattery and charm was all it took to own her soul.
Lusting for true love, she relinquished all control.
Craving outside approval, into his web she fell.
Swayed by infatuation, trapped under his spell.

Finally woken by reality, yet too late to break free.
He'd rather ignite her heart on fire than simply let her be.
Her world covered in ashes, as his lies burn her skin.
Get up or give up, the internal war she must win.

The beauty she relied on, stripped away by the fire.
Her worth in the world, must stem from a deeper desire.
Rebuilding self-esteem by conquering all she endured.
Confidence rebounding stronger, once justice is served.

Miss Pretty may have scars, but her beauty still burns bright.
When life tried to knock her down, she found the will to fight.
The strength she had to keep going was only just the start.
She rose above the fire and earned the name Braveheart.

About the Author

Jenn Sadai has combined her love of writing with her passion for empowering women into two inspiring series. The *Self-esteem Series* is comprised of four non-fiction stories that tackle various issues that impact women's self-esteem. *Dark Confessions of an Extraordinary, Ordinary Woman* delves into the dark consequences of domestic violence, drug use, and depression.

Dirty Secrets of the World's Worst Employee addresses bullying and sexual harassment in the workplace. *Cottage Cheese Thighs* combats every woman's battle with the scale. *No Kids Required* is the true stories of 20 trailblazing women who've chosen not to have children.

Her Own Hero was her first book in the fictional *Survivor Series* and it's an action-packed suspense that proves women have the power to save themselves. *Her Beauty Burns* is Katelyn from *Her Own Hero's* back story. There are six more strong characters from *Her Own Hero* that will get to share their own story in future additions to the *Survivor Series*.

Jenn Sadai is a proud Canadian, born in Windsor, Ontario, where she resides with her heroic husband and two lovable labs. Jenn can always be reached through the various social media links on her website, www.jennsadai.com.

Coming Soon

Jenn Sadai has a list of books she's working on, including the next book in the *Survivor Series*, *Her Elaborate Escape*. She is also working on a collection of stories from women who turned unimaginable tragedies into incredible triumphs entitled *Women Ready to Rise*.

CPSIA information can be obtained
at www.ICGtesting.com
Printed in the USA
LVHW030237280219
608997LV00002B/2